WHEEL OF AUGUSTUS

By Susan F. Banks

DEDICATION

To Michael and the usual suspects.

Thanks to Cherie Kephart for the alpha version edit and Marni Freedman for the beta version edit. This book would not have found its form without them.

Check out **susanfbanks.com** for the song list that accompanies this book.

LEGAL

Banks, Susan F. Wheel of Augustus. DG Fisher Publishing. Paperback Edition dgfisherpublishing@gmail.com

Cover Design: Ynne Black Art

'Soul never dies. Everything else is temporary.'

---- Gem, the Guardian of the Gate

CHARACTERS

Gem – Guardian of the Gate

Dora - the Hound of Hell

Jat the Deceiver – Lord of the Underworld

Circle of Augustus:

Willet Du Place – The Listener
Audrey Du Place – The Ring Thrower
Dean Simmons – The Golden Hearted Warrior
TJ Barlow – The Steel Warrior

The Teacher - Arhat Faroud Anselmi

The Traveler - Maria Sonrisa Degas de Megaro

The Zeemerites:

Lead Zeemer - Rollie Zeemer
Police Chief Edgar Zeemer,
Fire Chief Clarence Duggins,
Marine Major Chuck Tomasek

Supporters - Bart Johnson, James Jain, Nick Hardman

Books by Susan F Banks

Red Souls of the Underworld

Red Souls

Wall of Unknowing

Wheel of Augustus

The Listener Series

The Woman in the Wires

A State of Darkness

The creator of illusions and ruler of lost Souls is known by many names - Jat the Deceiver, Lord of the Underworld, Creator of Nightmares and Master of Despair. He seeks to control people, not through conquest, but through deception. His illusions trick the mind and enflame emotions.

Jat desires the city of Los Angeles for his own, to rule under his domain in the Underworld. He seeded the earth underneath Los Angeles with an insidious crystal that released swarms of Red Souls into the city. People became confused, despairing and lost. Walls of Unknowing covered the city to weaken their will and eliminate all resistance. Now L.A. teeters on the brink of an even darker future, the final descent into the Underworld.

HISTORY OF THE CIRCLE

The vibrational Gate between the physical world and the Underworld requires a Guardian. In Los Angeles, the Gate is guarded by a woman, named Gem. She has maintained it for over 170 years,. Gem is a Master of the Freezing Breath. The power of her breath calms negative emotions in people who have lost control, and it drives demonic invaders back into the Underworld. The Gate has been breached. It must be restored.

The Guardian raised an ancient fighting force, the Circle of Augustus, to join with her to close the breach in the Gate. She recruited four people from Los Angeles. They were unlikely recruits - two reclusive sisters, a rock musician and a real estate investor. Gem asked them to fight an enemy they couldn't see, for a purpose they didn't understand.

Accepting her request more on faith than certainty, their normal lives slipped away. When they finally saw the face of the Deceiver, they understood what they were fighting.

The Circle mounted an effective offense against Jat's previous attacks on the city. They decimated an underground crystal coming up through the ground before every building in L.A. was knocked over. They cleared the streets of Red Souls and sent them back to the Underworld. When a dragon-headed statue stood up and stepped off the roof of a ninety story building and trampled through the city on its huge stone feet, they stopped it in its tracks with hot energy rings that melted its head and feet.

Jat the Deceiver never rests. His newest ploy will be the Circle's biggest test yet.

Chapter 1

*****

Gem needed to speak to Augustus urgently. He had been her Teacher and Guide for nearly two hundred years. His counsel was essential. She found him in his office at Askleposis, the Temple of the High Astral. Augustus wore a white collared dress shirt without a tie. His snowy white hair was swept back off his face, and his white beard hung to his chest. Crisp creases lined the front of dove gray linen pants, and his feet were bare. He managed to look both serene and businesslike at the same time, and a calm white light emanated from him. He welcomed her with his usual smile of delight and love. "Welcome, my dear." He embraced her and kissed her on both cheeks. "To what do I owe this pleasure?"

Gem melted into his hug, letting his love ease some of the worry she carried on her shoulders. "We have a problem, Augustus. Los Angeles has gone dark, and the people are mired in Jat's trap. I need your guidance. What can I do to pull the city back from self-destruction?"

Augustus turned to a large rectangle of light suspended in midair in front of his desk. The Map of Consciousness on Planet Eart was a color-coded map of spiritual, mental and emotional heat across the globe. She had seen this amazing technology before. Thin blue lines demarcated the familiar boundaries of continents, islands and oceans. Land masses were green or brown, and the oceans and waterways were shades of blue and green. Areas in the north tended toward cooler colors. In the south, colors were warmer. On top of geologic structures, patches of color shifted and swirled with no regard for physical boundaries. Ridges of black surrounded areas of conflict. Yellow and orange patches pulsed like sores where tensions were high. Lines of hot red color shot out in stars where passions had erupted into violence.

Augustus moved his fingers over the map to zoom in on southern California. A smokey gray blot swirled over L.A. County where the Wall of Unknowing covered it. He touched the gray patch over Los Angeles on the map. Black lines spiked out under his finger. The map zoomed in closer on the dark streets where people fought each other with hands, bats and metal pipes.

"People forget their identity as Soul, their link with the Divine, but look here, it is not just Los Angeles. Other cities are at risk," he said, pointing to Phoenix, Sacramento and Las Vegas on the map. "See how they pulse orange, verging on red? Embers of emotion smolder there. If sparks of negativity fly out of Los Angeles, they will ignite those cities like kindling. People will act out in anger. Violence will take hold there as it has in your city."

Then a black star swelled on the map in the center of Los Angeles. His bushy white eyebrows rose. "The city is at the brink."

"What more can be done?" Gem's frustration showed, uncharacteristically, as gray shadows in her light body.

Augustus stroked the ends of his white mustache with thumb and forefinger and fixed his clear blue eyes on her. "Jat will try to take the city soon. There is still time for the Circle to turn the tide."

"How much time do we have?"
"A vanishingly small amount. Your Circle is under pressure. They are inside the Wall and not immune to its disorienting effects. If they cannot maintain their Light and inspire the Light in others, the city will be easily taken."

Gem's light body reacted with a red flush. "The Circle is not weak. They will not give in easily!"

"Do not underestimate Jat's ability to undermine the resolve of even the most focused fighters. Human beings have their emotional strings. He plays them to perfection. There is also the larger issue of what will happen to the space left behind if the city falls. It would leave behind a large discontinuity in spacetime. Time cannot progress in a vacuum, and the Earth Mother cannot tolerate such an anomaly in her realm. She will use her considerable powers to restore the physical place that disappeared so the continuity of time and space can resume."

"Whatever do you mean, Augustus."

Augustus drew a circle in blue on the map around Los Angeles County. "She will summon the Elemental Forces, King Ocean and Queen Desert. Ocean waters will wash the space clean, desert sand will cover it, and then Mother Earth will quickly begin to remake the land. She will not be gentle about it."

Gem stepped closer to peer at the map. "How would she do that?"

"With the physical forces of nature, my dear." Augustus put an arm around Gem's shoulders and walked with her toward an open wall of the office. "Mother Earth has many tools at her disposal. Earthquake, flood, fire - She will unleash them and let them have their way."

Gem shuddered and stepped back to look him full in the face. "What is the aftermath?"

"There will be no trace of what was there before."

"What about the Circle?" Gem said. "They have probably entered the city by now. What will happen to them while the city is remade?"

Augustus shook his head. A look of concern darkened his eyes. They walked outside and stood on a veranda looking over a large garden of rose bushes. "Members of the Circle must not be there when the remaking begins," Augustus said. "They will find themselves in a chaotic state of upheaval, much like the earliest days in the formation of the earth. Their physical lives will be forfeit."

Gem's brown eyes flashed with alarm. "They will think I deceived them and sent them to their death. They don't deserve that kind of end!"

Augustus' tone turned solemn. "Let the Circle know the limits of time, Guardian, before it is too late."

"What about the citizens of Los Angeles?"

"Every soul will move on to the world he or she has earned."

"Can we save them?"

"When Mother Earth rouses herself to action, the city will already be gone, along with everyone in it. Until then, have faith in the desire of people to be in Light rather than Darkness. Souls always have choice. They can resist the downward pull of the Underworld if there is the will to do so, but be warned, they are in Jat's domain now. He will fight with every weapon he knows."

Gem took a deep breath and hung her head. "I have never felt less equal to a task."

Augustus lifted her chin with a finger and looked into her eyes. "I believe in you, my dear. Find your strength and lead your Circle."

*****

Long shadows crossed the City of Angels like bars of a prison. A heavy fog full of static lightning lay over the city. It dulled human minds and killed memories. Fear and confusion had turned to violence in many areas. The beleaguered city languished in darkness, before the next step down into the new torments of a deeper hell. Chaos had taken over the streets. Such was the state of Los Angeles.

Jat the Deceiver's Dragon Head Building had appeared out of nowhere on the downtown L.A. skyline and replaced a bank building that had been there for decades. Standing ninety stories high, it looked dark and empty. The people of L.A. were so confused by the static of the Wall of Unknowing that no one thought twice about the building. They just accepted its sudden appearance. The building pulled on the city's energy like a black hole. The inner light in many people had snuffed out. They turned into astral skeletons. Other people managed to hold on to their light but had to hide from the skeletons or suffer awful attacks.

The Circle of Augustus wasn't sure how the building fit into Jat's plans. Willet, Audrey, TJ and Dean, fought two previous battles with Jat. They had stalled him for the moment, but now the demise of the city was imminent. The last instruction Gem, their leader, gave her Circle before she left them was, "Destroy the Dragon Head Building".

Gem had faced the Deceiver many times over her long tenure as Guardian of the Gate to the Underworld and defeated him every time. The Circle trusted her directions. She would never give them such a monumental task unless it were possible to fulfill it. Would she? Jat's creation pulsed with dark energy and had to be destroyed, but no one in the Circle wanted to go near it.

Every one of its ninety floors contained a nightmare. Willet and TJ had been inside and witnessed those nightmares firsthand. Willet saw a guillotine dripping blood off its blade into a basket with a head in it. "It was horrible," Willet recalled with a shudder. "It turns my stomach to think about it." TJ was trapped in a maze of burning lasers. He had the burn scars to prove it. "None of us should go there," he said.

Just entering the city and crossing through it would be a challenge. "We know what's out on the streets," Dean said. "Red Souls, Needle Men, spiders, berserkers. That's before we even get to the building. Maybe we should wait for Gem to get back."

Gem was their leader for a reason. Her unique power of Freezing Breath could repel any Underworld attacker. A hit of her icy breath neutralized negative emotions in people and stopped a panicking mob in its tracks. In short, she was irreplaceable in a fight.

"Gem told us to go in," Audrey said. "So, we throw up our Ring Light and sing HU like our lives depend on it, which they probably do." As the Circle's Ring Thrower, Audrey harnessed the positive energy of the Circle and used it to create rings of light on her fingers. She spun them until they get extremely hot and then hurled them at her chosen target. They rarely missed their mark and burned like hell.

"Someone has to deal with the building," Willet said. "If it's not us, who would it be?"

Could energy rings bring down a structure the size of the Dragon Head Building? They had never tried to cut through that much concrete, but they had been able to reduce Jat's underground crystal to charcoal. There was hope.

TJ was a real estate developer before he joined the Circle and had some experience with building demolition. He tried to apply what he knew to their problem. "We can't just blow up a building that size. Chunks of concrete would fly everywhere and kill people. The building has to be dropped. If we plant explosives around the base of it and jar the building just enough to undermine the foundation, then we throw Audrey's rings at the building to shake it loose. It will drop under its own weight, hopefully without a lot of flying debris. Pretty simple. We'll have to get people out of the area, of course."

"Hopefully? Pretty simple?" Dean said. "Where do you think we'll get explosives?"

"There's got to be explosives somewhere in L.A.," TJ said. "Do you have a better idea?"

"We just go to an explosives store," Audrey scoffed. "There's one on every corner."

"Optimism is needed right now, Auddie," Willet said. "Let's take cleansing breaths."

Audrey had grown irritable lately. The Ring Thrower had to spin and throw many energy rings in the course of their battles. She didn't always have time to recover her own strength. The other Circle members endured her moods with as much equanimity as they could, but they were getting a bit chippy too.

As the Circle's Listener, Willet's hearing is so acute she can hear voices speaking from far away and even from other planes. Her hearing acts as an early warning system for the Circle, but loud sounds give her incapacitating migraines. She's learning to control her inner ear vibrations. It's a work in progress.

Dean and TJ, the Circle's Warriors, provided muscle when needed and cleared obstacles from the Circle's path. The Dragon Head Building was a big obstacle.

The Circle stood on the balcony behind Griffith Park Observatory and watched Los Angeles lying in darkness beyond the mesa, covered by the Wall of Unknowing. The city, usually lit up and sparkling at night, was dark and paralyzed, awaiting its own death. Across the L.A. Basin, the shadow of the downtown skyline loomed like a hulking monster. The city appeared deserted, but there were people out there, suffering people. Wails of desolation and angry curses echoed through the streets. People wandered around in the dark, dispirited and angry, slowly regressing to the level of savages. The balance of energy had tilted away from Light. The Circle had to maintain their own connection to Light, or they would succumb to the same despair.

Each Circle member had been inside the Wall. They knew how dangerous it was. They would need all their strength and focus to go through it to reach the Dragon Head Building. The few energy bars left in their pockets had to sustain them. They ate every bar and wished there were more. Water would have been helpful. The water in the Griffith Observatory fountain was covered in murky green algae. They didn't dare drink it. A bout of intestinal distress would really slow them down

Then there was Dora, the faithful hound who protected the Guardian and fought at her side. Gem left Dora with the Circle to help them with their mission. The big black dog with the white patch on her forehead was no ordinary Labrador Retriever. She was the Hound of Hell. Her job was to send Jat back to the Underworld when he intruded on the physical world. Dora's ability to explode in size in a blaze of fire and energy was an awesome sight to behold. Having her with them was reassuring and welcome.

They watched Dora from a respectful distance. She sat on her haunches and blinked her big golden eyes at them, untroubled by their scrutiny. She would provide excellent backup, but how to communicate with her? Giving doggie commands seemed inappropriate. She was extremely intelligent. Who would dare put a leash on her, even if they had one? Dora knew what had to be done. The agenda came from the Guardian herself.

"What should we do?" Dean murmured. "Start walking and see if she follows?"

"Dora understands words," Audrey replied. "She probably knows what we're saying right now. We should just talk to her the way Gem does."

"Dora," Willet said, "We're have to go into the city now. Are you going to follow us? Or should we follow you."

Dora stood up on her long legs, stretched and shook in a vigorous spiral from head to tail, turned her back on them and sat down again facing the mesa.

TJ snorted and then tried to cover it with a cough. "Let's assume the dog will do what it needs to do," he said with thinly veiled sarcasm. "We should get going."

Willet shot him a raised eyebrow. "The *dog*? Really? Dora has saved our lives more than once. Anyway, what we need is a game plan. We've all been trapped in the Wall, we know what it's like, and we don't want to lose our minds and memories in the static. How are we going to remember each other and what we're supposed to do? We don't want to wander around like fools."

Everyone nodded, and Dora's ears twitched. Audrey fished inside her jacket pockets and pulled out a lipstick and a toll road receipt. "I'll write things down," she said. "Names, objectives..." She laid the paper on the palm of her hand and tried to write on it. "Nope, lipstick won't work. Have to find a pen...."

"Gem said L.A. is in an in-between state between the physical and astral," Willet said. "What we see and hear there will be different from what we see and hear on this mesa. Our senses will be different."

"The only rule I know is, we have to keep our lights on," TJ said. "Lots of HU chant. Otherwise, the Needle Men will be all over us." He closed his eyes, pictured the gray needle-fingered fiends swarming on top of him, heard the metal click of their needles, felt the sting when the needles pierced his flesh as if it was happening all over again. He shuddered.

Willet rubbed his arm. "I'm talking about how fast we move, how well we can see, what we can hear. We might have some degree of heightened perceptions. That would be an advantage if we can see what's coming."

"We can't trust everything we see and hear. I know that from experience.," TJ said. "You do too, Will. How will we know what's real and what's not?"

"Maybe Dora will give us a heads-up," Willet said, looking at the big dog. "She'll recognize Jat's deceptions before we do. I'm sure of it."

"Who's gonna lead this parade?" Dean asked. "Someone has to go first."

Why does it have to be one person?" TJ said. "We should go side-by-side."

"We can keep a better eye on what's around if we're single file," Dean said. "Eyes in all directions."

"Willet should go first since she has the best ears," Audrey said. "I'll follow her, and you guys flank us on each side. I'll throw up a light ring around all of us."

Dean nodded. "Sounds good, Strategas."

"I don't need your snark, Dean," she snapped. "I know how to organize teams. I do it for a living." Audrey had been especially prickly toward Dean lately. No one understood why, but the conversation degenerated from there.

"It wasn't snark. I said it sounds good, didn't I? No need to be touchy."

"I am *not* touchy." The pinched look on her face indicated otherwise. "Stop criticizing me."

"Ok, ok, we proceed single file," Willet said, trying to stem the tide of argument. "TJ, anything to add?"

"Nothing," TJ replied. "What about the dog?"

Willet glared at him. "If you mean *Dora*, she'll walk where she wants to walk, I suppose."

"Needle Men," TJ reminded them for the third time. "The demons with needles for fingers? They hurt like hell. Stay away from them."

"We're all aware of the Needle Men, Teej," Dean said. "No need to remind us again."

"I understand, sweetheart," Willet agreed. "I had needles in my eyes. It was horrible."

TJ huffed. "I had them in every muscle in my body. The pain was unbearable."

"Do we have to compare war stories right now?" Dean said. "We're already arguing, and we're not even in the city yet. We need harmony, or we won't make it out with our minds intact. Remember what we've been through together, why we're the Circle." He looked at each one of them for confirmation and got a mixture of nods and shrugs.

They sang a HU chant to center themselves and raise their consciousness. The air around them vibrated with the sound. When they finished, Dora stood up and slipped through a space between the pillars of the white balcony. She disappeared down the side of the mesa.

"I guess she's leading the way," Willet said. "Let's not lose her."

They all vaulted over the balcony and went slip-sliding down the embankment through sage, manzanita, creosote and cactus, trying to keep up with the long-legged dog. Dora moved fast and blended into the darkness. At the bottom of the mesa, they found Dora growling at the giant statue of the melted dragon headed man still cooling its heels there.

"I wish we blew up that damn statue before Jat got free of it," Audrey said.

Jat hid himself inside the statue and used it to travel across Los Angeles, crushing every building and street in its path. The Circle bombarded the statue with white-hot light rings until it stopped and left it to melt. They thought they had won a victory, but it was just a diversion. While they spent time stopping Jat's statue, the Walls of Unknowing covered all of Los Angeles County from desert to ocean and cut the city off from the rest of the world.

"I doubt that would have changed anything. No use crying over what-ifs," TJ said with a shrug.

"Who's crying?" Audrey scowled. "I'm not crying."

TJ tried diplomacy "I wasn't referring to you specifically. Can we get going now?"

The Circle lined up behind Willet, but Dora took position in front of her, and no one objected. The white spot on her forehead glowed like a headlight. Her upper lip curled, exposing her canines. The piercing light in her eyes said, 'stay out of my way'. They needed that.

Setting off across the mesa, they were soon stopped by a pack of coyotes that fanned out in a half-circle in front of them. The silver-gray of their fur set off the cold blue of their eyes. Dora gave a low, curdling growl that declared her dominance. The leader of the pack approached but kept a safe distance, glowing eye to glowing eye with the Hound, and then bowed down over front paws. Dora and the pack leader exchanged a series of growls, chuffles and whines, communicating in the common tongue of their ancestors. Dora raised her head, sniffed the air, and howled. The pack leader answered in kind, and the whole pack joined in a deafening howl. An agreement of some kind had been reached. The semicircle of coyotes parted and lined up on each flank, forming a wide arrow with Dora at the point. The Circle had a coyote escort.

They moved out of the halo of natural light that surrounded Griffith Park. It was the only area of L.A. that still had any. The park had been saved from total darkness by the presence of the Circle of Augustus. Its light extended to the edge of the mesa and then faded to black at the border where the netherworld of L.A. began. At that border, the coyote pack stopped and planted their front paws. The fur rose on their backs, and a howl went up. The pack would go no further. They fell back and scattered into the brush, leaving the Circle to continue on its own. Audrey threw a light ring in the air. It hovered over the Circle as they moved silently toward the dark city. Jat waited there. He knew they were coming. No one doubted that.

The temperature rose noticeably. The air smelled acrid. Erratic shafts of lightning ripped through the darkness, and shadows wavered in every corner. It was confusing to the eye and unsettling to one's sense of balance. Audrey's light ring spinning over their heads gave them welcome visibility. It also protected them from the worst of whatever hid in the darkness.

They formed a tight group under the light. Now that they were inside the boundary of L.A., they became linked in that wordless communication they had experienced before, hearing each other's thoughts as if they were spoken aloud. At least one pair of eyes scanned every direction for dangers. No one and nothing would take them unawares. The Circle entered the eastern part of Los Feliz, the neighborhood just south of Griffith Park. The streets seemed dead quiet.

"Do you hear anything, Listener?" Dean whispered. "Probably a silly question…"

"I hear arguments. Accusations, hot retorts, people on edge and afraid. Some are having sex. Sounds like the rough kind." Everyone stared at Willet. She shrugged. "You asked."

There were no lights in apartment windows, no streetlights, no traffic lights, no open businesses. "This is the most complete blackout I've ever seen," TJ said. "What happened to the electricity?"

"I'm surprised you'd even ask that question," Audrey said. "We're on the doorstep of the Underworld. I bet they don't have electricity there."

They walked past a group of four-plex apartments and heard a window open. Someone shouted curses. A second window opened, and another voice responded in kind. Soon a chorus of voices were cursing each other, trading insults and promising bodily harm. Windows banged shut abruptly, and the shouting match ended. Farther up the street, other voices took up the tirade. The Circle kept walking south and reached Thai Town. Buildings were on fire. People were climbing out of windows and hanging from ledges and fire escapes, facing long drops to the ground. Others escaped through ground floor doors lugging armfuls of belongings. Smoke billowed through the air. Black-hooded gangs with bats and shovels smashed at anything made of glass and set cars on fire. Shadows chased the few people daring to be outside. They ran for their lives.

"A lot of desperate praying out there," Willet said. "Mumbling about revenge and End of Days. People are preparing for the worst.."

"Let's move," TJ said, taking her hand. "This is s a war zone."

Farther south in Little Armenia, it got quiet again, but the darkness vibrated in very faint shades of color. Nothing looked truly solid. Even the black sky, slate-colored sidewalks, and cadet gray of the buildings looked like smeared watercolors. It was easy to get dizzy. People out on the streets were bundled in dark clothes despite the heat. Hints of dull gold, gray sage and dusk rose glimmered off slivers of exposed skin, casting haloes of subtle color on their shoulders.

"What do you hear now, Listener?" Dean asked.

Willet cocked her head to the side and closed her eyes. "The colors are humming. Even shades of black have a ring to them. People are whispering in different languages. Don't know what they're saying or if they're talking to each other. Maybe just talking to themselves."

Dean bounced lightly on his feet. "Do you feel that? The concrete. It feels spongy. Not solid."

The rest of the group tested the ground and had to agree. Concrete was not supposed to feel that way.

Dean then touched the top of a blue mailbox. His fingers merged into the surface of the metal. He felt a sharp tingle in his skin, and his fingers turned cold and heavy. It began to hurt. He pulled his hand away quickly. The fingers vibrated bluish for a few seconds before returning to a normal color. "It felt like my hand was becoming part of the mailbox, turning into metal," he said, rubbing his fingers. "In the physical world, we know where the boundaries between objects are. Here, the boundaries between objects are blurred. Kind of cool to experience it, but it's painful."

"What does that mean?" Willet said.

"It's all a continuum of waves. At a certain level, everything is energy. Nothing is actually solid. That fact might help us when we reach the Dragon Head."

"Why is that, oh physics god?" Audrey said. "Pray tell us."

Dean reacted to her tone. "What is your problem? Did I say something to offend you? Again?"

"Well, excuse me, professor. I guess the rest of us don't understand what you're implying."

You're a computer engineer, Audrey," Dean said. "You've studied physics. What I say should make sense to you."

"I don't remember studying anything that suggested we could become part of a mailbox."

Red sparks flashed like fireworks around Audrey. Dean's aura turned an angry orange red in response. Willet turned yellow, and a greenish gold tint surrounded TJ. Everyone's emotions were color coded and visible to all.

"Uh oh," TJ chuckled. "No way to hide now."

Dora sat on her haunches, watching them. Her black fur and white forehead patch shimmered with energy, and the baleful expression in her gold eyes said, "When will you people be done bickering?"

Dean summoned his self-control and took a deep breath. "If nothing is truly solid," he said, "that means we could break the Dragon Head Building apart if we have the right leverage."

Another verbal battle broke out in a nearby apartment complex. F-bombs and insults flew from open windows, blistering the air with threats. "You stink… Your mother… Stupid shit…" New voices joined in, louder, trying to drown out the others. The streets felt on edge, about to explode, and the tension was affecting the Circle. The light around them weakened along with their unity. They started to become forgetful.

Long shadows slithered around the periphery of the Circle's ring light. The clicking of needle fingers echoed in the gloom. "That's them," TJ whispered. "The Needle… things."

"What Needle things?" Willet said.

"Turn up the light, and let's get going," Dean muttered. "Before their waves cancel out our waves, and we all flatline. Do you think you can do that for us, Audrey, please?"

Audrey looked at her fingers, fumbled, and then finally spun another ring on her index finger. She stared at it a moment and then tossed it above their heads. The ring settled around their shoulders with a glow that reinforced their previous ring. The Needle Men melted away into darker corners. A crisis averted, but the Needles would await another opportunity to attack.

Chapter 2

Corporal Nickel Hardman, ex U.S. Army, and James 'Boulevard' Jain sat on a sidewalk next to the parking lot of a demolished grocery store in East Hollywood that had been crushed by the dragon-head statue's rampage. They never did find their car. The city went dark, and they barely saw hands in front of their faces. It was useless to get up and try to go anywhere, so they just sat there, waiting for lights to turn on. After twenty minutes, nothing had changed. After thirty minutes, they started to make plans. After an hour of darkness, they changed those plans. The only hint of light came through the weave of the burlap bag Nick held in his lap. They had taken the bag from Dean and Audrey when they 'borrowed' their car. Nick opened the mouth of the bag, and a halo of white light burst out as strong as a streetlamp. The bag was full of crystal pieces sparkling like diamonds. It shocked their light-deprived eyes and made them water.

"Are you sure we should have this stuff?" Jain asked as he peered in the bag. "It destroyed our apartment, remember?"

Nick thought about the first time he met Audrey. Her skin glowed green as a neon light. "The crystal made Audrey turn green. When I touched her, she shocked me like a live wire. We need light. The crystal packs a lot of power, JJ. You're not afraid of these little sparkly pieces, are you?" he said, waving the bag under his friend's nose.

"I'm not afraid of anything'," Jain said, waving the bag away. "Remember who you're talkin' to."

Nick knew full well who he was talking to. He and Jain had known each other since boyhood when they ran in the same neighborhood in L.A. Jain protected Nick on the rough streets. When Nick's mother died and Nick's father abdicated parental responsibility in a haze of alcohol, Jain's Mama unofficially adopted him. Nick eventually joined the army, went to Afghanistan, and was hit by a roadside bomb. He came back to the U.S. with a bad case of PTSD, his chest and legs riddled with shrapnel. It was Jain who brought him home and took care of him. Nick would do anything for Jain. They were brothers in every way that mattered.

The bag of crystal shed a nimbus of light around them. It attracted attention. People walked into the parking lot and approached in ones and twos. Their bodies flickered like x-rays just under the skin, a skeletal appearance like the afterimage of a flash camera. As they entered the halo of crystal light, their skeletal appearance faded. A young Asian woman, ghostly pale, carried a baby wrapped in dark blue blanket. The baby's thin hair was black and pin-straight, and its little fists were curled up tight. The woman approached, crouched in front of Nick and held out her hand. He pulled a small piece of crystal from the bag and placed it on her palm. The color of her skin warmed. She touched the crystal to her baby's cheek. The baby turned pink gold, threw its chubby arms up in the air and giggled, and the woman smiled. Other people shuffled closer and knelt. Nick began to hand out small pieces of the crystal to everyone who approached, like a cleric giving benedictions.

Jain took a piece, and then whispered, "Dude, don't give it all away. It's our only light."

Nick nodded but kept giving pieces to whoever held out a hand. Soon, the light spread out to the four corners of the city block. It was a good thing. Just beyond the light, shadows swept across the ground and up the sides of buildings. The shadows slid to the border of the halo and then withdrew from the light as if repelled.

Jain leaned toward Nick and murmured in his ear. "Those shadows are getting closer. What's up with that?"

"Probably hazardous to our health," Nick said. "Just a guess."

*****

Audrey had given Bart Johnson a few pieces of crystal when TJ first found them at his club after it burned down. That seemed like years ago. Bart discovered he could grow them. Pieces of the crystal planted in dirt multiplied and spread like weeds, producing enormous amounts of light. More importantly, he and Dean found that the crystal repelled a Wall of Unknowing. The Wall never encroached on Bart's fields as it spread across L.A. Dean told him to grow as much crystal as possible and have it ready to defend the city.

Now Bart stood at the edge of his fields now and looked out at what he could see of Los Angeles, dark and defenseless, and greatly in need of light. The time had come to test the crystal's power on a large scale. There were questions. Could he harvest enough of it to make a difference against the enormity of the Wall? What exactly was he supposed to do with it? How would he transport it? Bart had a pickup truck with a slatted wooden enclosure on the truck bed. He shoveled crystal from the fields into twenty-five-pound burlap bags and loaded the bags into the back of the truck until the suspension almost groaned. It seemed an insignificant amount to save a city as large as L.A, but it was the best he could do. He drove the truck to the edge of his property. The Wall of Unknowing rose to the sky like a dark static-spitting monster just across the road. There was a freeway on the other side, but he couldn't see it through all the static and spikes of lightning. If he wanted to bring the crystal to Dean, he would have to cross the road into the Wall and find the freeway, driving blindly. He heard engines rev and horns honk inside all the roiling gloom. Using the sounds as a guide, he rolled the truck very slowly forward. The static swallowed him. He felt the onramp rise under his tires and let the truck edge up as carefully as a blind driver could. Then he merged into what he hoped was the slow lane of the freeway. Lightning flashed in zip-zags, and the hiss of static washed out other sounds. Traffic blew past at speeds he could feel from the waves of air hitting the side of his truck. *How are they driving so fast with so little light?* He chugged along in the slow lane, hoping the faster moving vehicles would just pass him by. His tires rolled over the chunky debris. Felt like car parts. Previous collisions? No surprise that accidents were happening. He didn't want to be stranded inside the Wall with a wrecked truck.

The radio was still tuned to the station he and Dean had listened to on their previous trip. Through the barrage of static, he heard a scratchy voice.

"Stay out of central L.A. For the safety of you and your loved ones, do not go downtown. A giant has stampeded through the city. The streets are reduced to rubble. Repeat, stay out of central L.A. for your own good."

Has that guy been drinking? Bart said out loud.

"No, I have not been drinking," the radio voice said. "This is your sober friend, Richard Theese."

Bart stepped on the gas until the truck rattled. He wondered if he'd be able to see the exit to the park when he came to it. If a giant destroyed the streets, how would he reach Dean and Audrey? They probably needed the crystal right away. He had to find them, despite the recommendations of his friend, Richard Theese.

*****

The dragon headed statue's large, heavy feet left deep holes in the streets when it stomped through the city, full of broken concrete, dirt, rebar, and glass. People couldn't see them and fell in and impaled themselves on something sharp. Their anguished cries echoed in the darkness. Jain had to admit the light of the crystal came in handy. He and Nick could see clearly in case anyone or anything came up on them unawares. Even though Nick was giving tiny pieces away to anyone who asked, they still had three quarters of a five-pound bag left. Someone had the bright idea of grabbing clear plastic cups from the nearest grocery and putting crystal chips in them, which magnified the light. Nick dropped crystal chips into the cups. The street around the parking lot lit up like a festival, and the mood lifted. It seemed to drive away the shadows that crawled over buildings just beyond the light.

No one rushed at Nick or tried to grab the bag. Nevertheless, Jain stood behind him and played his usual role as the muscle, protecting both friend and bag. He wanted to make sure there was something left of the crystal for him and Nick after everyone else got a piece. The soft clicking noise coming out of the shadows gave him the creeps. Something in there was watching and waiting. For now, everyone held on to their little cups of light and huddled together. It was nice, almost happy, but it was not to last.

The sound of marching feet approached from around the block, and suddenly, everyone scattered, leaving Nick and Jain alone on the curb. Nick tied a hasty knot in the burlap bag of crystal. Jain grabbed the bag and stuffed it inside his leather jacket. A small pack of quasi-military men in black uniforms rounded the corner and marched up to them. They had black dragon insignia on the chests and silver stripes on their arms and stopped on a cue from the guy up front who raised his hand.

"Illegal production of light was reported in this area," he said. "You will come with us now."

"Since when did light become illegal?" Jain protested, stepping in front of Nick. "You can't arrest us for that."

"Zeemers will be arrested on sight, by order of his honor the Mayor. They are a menace to our society and are considered outlaws."

"We're not Zeemers," Jain said, and looked at Nick for confirmation.

"We don't even know who they are!" Nick exclaimed.

"I am authorized to detain you and bring you to headquarters at the Dragon Head Building where you will be interrogated." The man spoke in a monotone. He motioned to someone behind him who stepped forward with ropes in each hand. That looked ominous.

Nick scrambled up from the curb. He and Jain turned and ran, only to be hit in the back with a paralyzing shockwaves that brought them to their knees. The soldiers looped ropes around their necks and pulled them taut. They were led away. After a couple of blocks, they met another contingent of soldiers who had their own line of roped prisoners in tow. Nick and Jain were leashed to the end of that chain and the line marched on. After several more blocks of forced march, Nick whispered into Jain's ear from behind. "Do you still have the bag in your jacket?"

"Yeah," Jain said out of the corner of his mouth.

"If I get my hands free, can I get at it and pull it out?"

"Maybe. If you don't tickle me."

"Don't be a dope. This isn't funny."

"Those stun guns look weird. And don't call me a dope."

"Be cool and focus," Nick said. "I have a knife in my pocket."

"How does that help?"

"It can cut the ropes, genius."

The guards were rather lax in their observation of the prisoners, proving they were more Rent-A-Cop than an elite fighting force. Half the guards walked up front, and half walked behind. None of them seemed to watch the line. Nick had practiced escape tactics in the Army. He managed to loosen the ropes around his wrists and wriggle out of them, keeping his wrists faux-wrapped. He slipped one arm slowly forward around Jain's waist, finding the edge of the leather jacket, reached in for the bag and eased it out. When he had secured the bag, he slipped the knife out of his pocket and handed it around to Jain. "Cut yourself free. Be cool about it."

"I was born cool." Jain took the knife, freed his wrists, and sliced through the rope connecting his neck to Nick's. He cut himself free of the prisoner in front of him and put the knife in his pocket. "What now?"

Nick slipped him a handful of crystal chips. He dug another handful of chips out of the bag. It was unfortunate to have to waste them, but there was no help for it. "Throw chips at the guards and take off running. I'll hit the ones at the back of the line. When the forward troops turn around, you hit them with your chips. Aim for their faces. We'll bolt, hopefully before they can aim their stunners."

It was one of Nick's more risky plans, but they had to do something before they ended up in a place with no escape. Jain readied the chips in his palm. Nick spun around and threw his handful at the guards behind him, then bolted. The guards started shouting, their faces smoked, and the guards in front turned to look. Jain threw his chips at them with all the old football strength he still had in his arm and took off after Nick. They cleared a city block. The sound of pounding boots approached loud and clear from behind. It would be hard to outrun those guys. Once again, they needed a vehicle for a real escape.

"Always without wheels," Jain grumbled. "I'm so tired of it.'

*****

Bart pulled the truck to the shoulder of the freeway and stopped. Driving in lightning-shredded darkness wasn't working. He couldn't read the freeway signs. He got out, found his way to the back of the truck by feel, and unlocked the back hatch, took out his trusty seed blower from its hook, and loaded the canister with crystal pieces from one of the bags. When the blower felt full in his hands, he aimed it up and shot a small spray of crystal into the air. The darkness lit up. His brain lit up too. *Always knew the crystal was special. I could make a fortune with this stuff.* With better light, he saw traffic racing by in the lanes next to him. On the other side of the freeway, traffic was bumper-to-bumper going east. Cars drove on the shoulders to get around snarls. Motorcycles weaved through the gridlock. Impatient honks blared, and rev'd engines growled. There was a guy on a bicycle in the fast lane. Everyone was fleeing the city by any means possible.

Bart circled the truck and sprayed a few chunks of crystal on his hood. It didn't take much. The pieces glittered with light. Crystal dust sparkled in the air like snow in moonlight and illuminated the road. Some vehicles were stopped in freeway lanes, unable to proceed because they had no headlights. He suspected someone would see his light and try to grab the blower and bags of crystal or carjack the whole truck. He did a hasty reload of the blower, locked up the hatch, and dashed for the driver door. He heard a car door open. Sure enough, a medium height muscular guy in a black muscle tee shirt and jeans came around the front of a stalled jeep and stalked slowly towards him. Crystal light reflected off studs piercing his eyebrows, nose, lip and ears. Grim determination burned in his eyes. Bart climbed in the cab and pulled the blower in with him. The blower was so bulky, he couldn't get the door fully closed, but he gunned the engine and took off as fast as the truck would allow, looking back to see if the big guy would run after him. Sure enough, the guy jumped on the back bumper and rattled the slats of the enclosure. The slats were sturdy but still just made of wood, and the bags were too big to fit between them. The guy pounded his fist on the wood, trying to crack it. He succeeded. Bart heard a crack and then a 'woop'. He hit the gas harder and saw the guy drop off the back bumper holding one of the bags under his arm with a victorious fist in the air.

That jerk! I'll have to fix the slat before anything else falls out. Can't lose any more crystal.

Bart rested the blower across his lap and aimed the blowing end out the driver window. He fired a short burst of crystal ahead of him every couple of minutes and picked up speed. The illumination allowed him to proceed at about thirty-five miles per hour with decent visibility. When a sign came into view, he had to slow down and aim a stream at it so he could read it. He wouldn't get anywhere fast at this rate, but it was better than nothing.

Eventually, the blower emptied. He needed to reload. He pulled off the freeway at the next exit and stopped, examining the broken slat hanging on the back of his trailer. *Damn, I need new wood and nails.* He filled the canister with more crystal and released a short stream into the air to see where he was. A stand of dead trees nearby showed the withering effects of the Wall. A row of small houses down the road sat in complete darkness. A dog growled low. He heard children crying. They sounded scared. It was a sound he couldn't ignore.

He walked down the road to the houses and sprayed a long, thick line of crystal at the edge of the small yards in front of the houses. Suddenly, there was light. Adults, children, dogs and cats who huddled inside or on porches rushed out to examine the source of light, stared and poked fingers in the crystal.

"This light will last a long time," Bart told them. "If you take pieces into your homes, they'll shine better than light bulbs. I can only leave you this much. Don't waste it." He walked back to his truck. Excited voices burst out behind him, and dogs yelped. Delighted conversations bubbled. Instead of children crying, he heard their laughter. A win on this insane journey.

He rolled the truck back to the freeway, headed west, and began to see signs for Dodger Stadium. *I can get to Griffith Park from there.* It had been a while since he'd come all the way into the city. He took an off ramp that ended up on Sunset Boulevard. It didn't seem to be as dark as it was when he first entered the Wall. Maybe his eyes had adjusted. *The sun was up when I left the farm. Is it still daytime?* In this low light, streetlights would normally switch on, but there was no electric light anywhere.

Smudges of color moved among drifting shadows. People walked inside the shadows. He was so fascinated by it that he almost couldn't stop the truck in time to avoid hitting two men in the middle of the street jumping and waving their arms at him, yelling for help. The air flushed red around them, and ropes hung around their necks. He considered driving away until he saw the uniformed guards running toward them from down the street.

The two men quickly climbed onto the running board on the passenger side of the truck and opened the door. "You gotta help us," a black guy in a leather jacket said, breathless as he slid into the passenger seat. "Those jackasses think they have the right to arrest us for having light."

The sandy-haired white guy climbed in after him, wearing military fatigues with "Hardman" stenciled on his shirt pocket. "Back up, fast, go the other way," he said. "If they zap your truck with those guns, the engine will blow up."

On instinct, Bart threw the truck in reverse and hit the gas hard. The truck groaned and sped backwards. Fortunately, there was no traffic behind him. "This isn't a high-performance vehicle," Bart said. "If I turn too fast, it might tip over." He kept his foot pressed to the gas, driving straight backward until he was several blocks from the guards, and then made as sharp a left turn as he dared. He headed down a side street, made another left and then a right, looking for a freeway or some big street he could use to make a faster getaway. "Tell me what's going on, before I stop and throw you out of my truck."

"That big honking statue almost stepped on us, and everything went dark," the military guy said. "We couldn't find our car and had to run for our lives."

"I heard about the statue on the radio," Bart said. "That was real?"

"As real as broken bones," leather jacket guy said. "And then those goons arrested us for making light. Can you believe that? My name's Jain, by the way. This is Nick. Thanks for helping us out."

Something about those words rang a bell in Bart's mind. "How do you make light?"

Nick pulled the half-full bag of crystal out of his shirt and opened it. The light of the crystal lit up his face.

"Geezzus," Bart spluttered. "Where did you get that?"

"A guy named Dean had it, and a lady, Audrey. It made her turn green," Jain said. "They went to Griffith Park to do something, but then the statue started walking toward the park and everything hit the fan." He rubbed at the top of his head. "We ran the other way. It was crazy."

Unbelievable. "Dean and Audrey?" Bart said. "When was the last time you saw them?"

 "They were still at the park when we left," Nick said. "That was yesterday afternoon. We borrowed their car, sort of. You know them?"

"I'm going to Griffith Park to find them. They better be ok," Bart said, giving the two men a cold-eyed stare.

"We didn't do a thing to them!" Jain said. "But you don't want to go to the park, dude. The monster was walking that way. You need to go the other direction! That thing's like a steamroller."

Jain and Nick gave Bart the details on the chaos and damage caused by the dragon headed statue. Bart wasn't sure he believed anything they said, but it corroborated what Richard These reported on the radio. He also wasn't sure if going to the park was the best thing to do, but he had to chance it if Dean and Audrey were there. He hoped the suspicious ride-alongs wouldn't complicate things.

"Look," Nick said. "I feel like me and J owe Dean for taking his car, and I really wanna make sure the lady is ok. If you take us with you, we'll give you all the backup we can give. I'm ex-army, you can count on me, and Jain's an expert in the L.A. streets. He'll get you there fastest, plus he's a tough fighter."

Audrey. If she was in trouble, Bart had to find her, even if it meant getting in the way of a stampeding stone giant. These two guys saw the statue firsthand. That might be useful. They knew about the crystal. The coincidence was too weird. Some things happened for a reason. He was learning that. He threw the truck in reverse, swung around and headed for Griffith Park as fast as the rattling truck would move.

Chapter 3

Sunset Boulevard cut through the heart of Hollywood, the playground of goth ghouls and flamboyant freaks on a normal day. Today was no different, except everything looked different. The street had the blurred look of an impressionist painting on a rainy day with none of the charm. The Circle had to squint to figure out what they were seeing. The air felt sluggish. Threads of lightning cut through the fog and static of the Wall of Unknowing. The few people who were out on the streets showed glimmers of color on exposed skin – blues, gray-greens and bronzes. Despite the heavy air, they pulled up their collars and hoods and pulled on gloves, seeming to want to hide their colors. The reason soon became apparent.

The Circle made their way down the boulevard in tight formation within the circumference of their ring of light. The city had become a film noir movie. Loose-jointed skeletons ambled down the street, their bones glowing dull silver inside black auras. Pedestrians crossed the street to avoid getting too close and huddled deeper into their coats to hide their colors. They couldn't hide completely. A thin sliver of amber escaped from the chin of one passerby. A skeletal figure ran at the man from behind and grabbed him by the arm, then poked him in the ear with a boney finger. The man recoiled, raised his voice in protest and tried to throw a punch. His fist passed right through the nebulous aura around the skeleton. An echoing laugh came out of the skeleton's boney jaws. Other skeletons appeared out of the darkness and surrounded the man. They tripped him when he tried to get away and knocked him to the sidewalk. The skeletons kicked him in the face and stomach repeatedly until the man didn't move. Then they sauntered away, leaving the man lying where he fell.

The Circle crossed the street to check on him. He was young, dishwater-blonde hair with scraggly beard. He was clutching his stomach. Audrey knelt beside the man and put her hands on his stomach. The light of her fingers seemed to have a soothing effect on the pain in his abdomen. He heaved a sigh. His eyelids fluttered. When he squinted up at them, his watery blue eyes popped wide open. "What the…" He scooted backward on his heels and elbows in a crab walk. "Are you crazy? Cover your lights! You'll get us all arrested!" The man dragged himself up to standing with painful effort.

"You're injured," Audrey said. "You need to go to a hospital."

The man laughed. "You're kidding, right? There's no hospital open around here. The Mayor's Guards will be all over us if they see us lit up like this. Thanks for the tune-up and all, but I'm out of here." He turned and staggered down the street still clutching his stomach.

"Hey," TJ called after him. "You don't know where we could buy some dynamite, do ya?"

"What Mayor's Guard is he talking about?" Dean said.

"That would be my old pal, Matt Gregg," TJ said sourly. "He was calling himself Mayor of L.A. last time I saw him. He had his Guards arrest me and lock me in the laser room, that horse's ass. I'd like to get my hands on him again."

"Focus, dude, focus," Dean reminded him. "We can't let old grudges sidetrack us."

The sidewalks leading away from their position were all broken. Large wedges of crystal had cracked through the concrete after Jat the Deceiver's first attack on L.A. At this point, no one cared enough to clean anything up. That included the dead bodies that were left behind. They noticed a body lying in the middle of the street and stopped short.

Conflicting thoughts pinged among them. "What should we do?" "He looks dead." "What if he isn't?" "We should check." The light was too dim to make out much from where they stood, so they walked into the street for a closer look. What remained of their ring light illuminated the body of a man with his head bashed in on the left side, a mess of blood and bone fragments in his brown hair and a vacant stare in his brown eyes. Definitely dead.

"The poor man." "We're getting distracted, have to keep going." "Where are we going again?"

Staying focused on the task at hand was becoming more difficult. The cohesion of the Circle frayed. Audrey's moods swung between fretful and combative. No one could say a word to her without a sharp retort. TJ got impatient, and Dean maintained a stony silence.

Willet remained the calm center. She drew Audrey aside, hugged her close, and whispered in her ear. "What's the matter with you, Auddie? You're bitching at everyone."

"I'm not bitching."

"You're snapping at us."

"I never snap!" Audrey snapped.

Willet took her sister's hands in hers. "Your hands are ice cold." Odd considering the warm temperature. She gave them a vigorous rub.

Audrey shivered under her sister's touch. "I don't know what's going on with me, Will. My insides feel hollowed out and I can't calm down. I wish I had a couple of Agnes' tranquilizers right now."

"Just what you don't need. Do you want to get like Mom?"

A confused look washed over Audrey's eyes. "Why would I be like Mom?"

No point in pursuing that conversation. If Audrey already forgot what they were talking about, what was the point? Her short term memory seemed to be failing.

Anxious thoughts came from Dean and TJ. "What's happening? Everything ok?"

"I'm having an anxiety attack or something," Audrey said with a visible shudder. "I don't know what I'm doing."

Dean came to her and wrapped his arms around her. "I'm sorry. You were really sensitive to the Wall's influence when we were in it. I should have expected a strong reaction from you this time."

"My nerves are shot, Dean. When will this be over? I want to go home."

Dean hugged her tighter. "We all agreed, remember? The Musketeers, all for one? We were in your kitchen when *you* asked us to commit. It'll be over after we topple the Dragon Head."

She pulled back and gave him a puzzled look. "I'm not sure what you're talking about, but it's always something, isn't it," she said in a dull voice. "Crisis after crisis. Eventually there'll be nothing left of our lives. Just fighting."

"We love you, Auddie," Willet said. "Everything feels like a struggle right now. We're all dealing with it."

"And we need you," TJ said. "A lot. I wish I didn't have to bring up the obvious, but you've got the rings. We won't be able to take down the building without you."

Audrey covered her face with her hands, and then she looked up. "The rings, yes. And the building. What is that again? It had a name..."

Audrey was definitely losing her memory faster than the rest of them. Maybe it was because of the energy she had to expend to spin her rings. No one said a word for fear of rattling her. She did manage to spin up a ring. They could see it was weaker than it had been. The Circle contributed as much of their own energy as they could and re-organized into a square behind Dora. TJ and Willet walked shoulder to shoulder, and Dean and Audrey walked behind them, holding hands. Their solidarity energized the ring. Its light pushed the shadows further away. Just in time.

An amorphous pitch-dark shape appeared a few blocks down Sunset Boulevard. It stood out against the lesser dark of the surroundings and floated in their direction. Skeletons and pedestrians alike moved aside to let it pass. The Circle stopped and stood firm. The dark shape picked up speed. The closer it got, the bigger it looked, big enough to swallow them. The darkness came to a stop within a yard of the Circle. It seemed to pull on the light ring, testing its strength. The ring held, but each member of the Circle felt a painful tug in the heart center, like hope being ripped away. The velvet darkness thinned, revealing three men and a woman standing inside it. The woman stepped forward and confronted the Circle with a bold stare. Her exotic looks suggested a mixed heritage, Filipino, Asian, maybe Pacific Islander, with the distinct hint of the supernatural. Everything about her demanded attention. Long black hair draped her shoulders. The look in her dark eyes was hot and cold the same time, and her sensuous red lips curled in a smirk. The skin-tight tiger print jumpsuit she wore swam over her body. It was dizzying if one stared too long. Her spiked heels and long fingernails were fire engine red.

Two bald white men, bare-chested and in leather breeches, stood behind her with rings in their ears and noses and studs in their lips. They had the stolid look of weightlifters and the dull glare of professional killers. They held heavy wooden clubs studded with iron spikes in their meaty fists. They looked as if they had just walked out of the Carpathian Mountains to terrorize the townspeople. The men brandished their clubs toward the Circle. The third man was tall and black, wearing black ninja attire with a black scarf tied around his head. His clothes hung loose on his tall frame giving him plenty of room to move. A long sword balanced on his left shoulder. He kept his hand on the hilt.

The woman raised her chin and showed straight white teeth that seemed too big for her mouth. She pointed at Dora. "You dare bring such a beast into our territory? We do not like your light. It is a provocation."

TJ nudged Willet behind him with his left arm and took a step forward, staying within the light ring. "This is a public street," he said. Sudden constriction in his chest made it hard to breathe, but he tried to sound neutral. Dean came up beside TJ and took position at his right shoulder. "We're just passing through," he said. "If you don't mind."

The woman eyed them and laughed. "You carry no weapons," she said. "What will you do if my men bury the spikes of their clubs in the beast's brain? Will you cry for your lost baby?"

No one in the Circle knew how Dora would respond to the threat, but they figured she would do something. "This dog is unpredictable," Dean said. "You should worry about your own brains, if you have any."

The woman snorted and stepped aside. The two big guys came forward to challenge Dora with heavy arms holding the clubs over their heads, their grins full of yellow, broken teeth. Dora's jaws snapped open. Fire blasted out of her mouth and hit the men square in the face and chest. The blast came so quick that it was too late for the men to avoid the flames. Their clubs caught fire, and the spikes melted. The men dropped the clubs and covered their faces and bald heads with scorched hands. Exposed skin burned blazing red and began to bubble. They fell back on their butts, screaming.

The woman looked at Dora in astonishment and nodded. "A manifestation of great power. I want this beast, Benzán."

The tall shadowy man in black slid closer to her. He swung the sword off his shoulder and pointed it at the Circle. "What Lady G wants Lady G shall have." He stared at him. His black eyes glittered "We will take the animal."

The Circle's ring light flared and sprayed the Shadow Man with sparks. His dark aura swallowed them. He laughed and thrust his sword in Dora's direction. Dora's mouth opened again. She blasted him with a white flame even hotter than the fire she used on the two big men. Shadow Man was incinerated. Ashes drifted to the ground leaving nothing behind but smoke.

Silence followed. What was there to say after that annihilation? "Uh, Good dog," Dean offered.

Dora sat back, scratched at her right ear with her hind paw, and heaved a smokey sigh. She had made an impression. In this netherworld Los Angeles, the Hound of Hell was supreme.

The bald men had rolled to their feet and taken off running down the street and around a corner, out of sight. That left the woman standing there alone, staring at Dora. She didn't seem bothered or fearful. "I need new men," she said, sizing up TJ and Dean. "You will do. Bring the beast. The women can leave us."

Thoughts pinged around the Circle. "Is she serious?" "She's nuts." Audrey managed to put extra 'uumph' into the light ring. It spun faster and threw off a fountain of sparks that showered the woman.

"We have places to be," TJ said. "No time to join your posse, sorry."

"Ah, but you will find me so inviting, tall one," she said. "And you," she turned to Dean. Her sharp eyes appraised him. "Handsome. You are not mated. There is nothing to hold you."

Dean's eyes narrowed. "You're not my type."

Audrey's aura turned bruise purple. She moved in next to Dean and spun a ring around the two of them. "Take a hint, Vampira," she said. "Get lost."

Willet came to Audrey's side. "What the Ring Thrower is trying to say is there's no room in here for you, and no one's coming out to join your team."

The woman studied the light ring and then reached out a hand. Her dark aura sizzled when she touched the ring, one trying to consume the other, but the ring whined like a table saw and sliced the nails off three of the woman's fingers. She yanked her hand to her chest and cradled it, glaring at them. "You have marred me," she snarled. "Do you know how difficult it is to get a good manicure in this city? The insult will not go unpunished."

Audrey sneered. "I haven't begun to insult you. Let's start with those ridiculous shoes you're wearing. I bet they kill your feet," she said, just warming up to a verbal barrage.

Dean put his arm around her. "OK, babe, I think you've made your point. Time to leave."

Dora rose to her feet. She seemed restless. The woman stepped back, giving the Hound plenty of space. She studied her broken fingernails for a moment and then gave the Circle a sweet smile that showed all her teeth. "There, there, no need for a tiff. My name is Georgina. You may call me Lady G. Everyone does. I admire your capabilities and this amazing beast with you. Perhaps you'd like to accompany me to my club. We could share a glass of something and become better acquainted. Wonderful music is played there. You would be my guests."

This turnaround in attitude confused the Circle. Colors of mustard, celery and taupe flickered in their auras, except for Audrey who spiked red and snickered. "I'm not calling you 'Lady' anything."

Dean's eyes flickered with interest. "Music? What kind of music?"

"It is music of great power, brutal and glorious. It would appeal to you, I think," Lady G said, giving Dean an intense stare. "Come with me."

"We're on our way downtown," TJ said. "No time for a club date."

"Go away," Willet said. Audrey had light rings spinning on all of her fingers.

Lady G ignored the sisters. "My club is just down the street. You could stop in for a moment and then be on your way. What is the harm in that?" She purred with charm.

Dean murmured in TJ's ear. "We might hear something fresh. I could use it in the band. It wouldn't slow us down more than a minute. What *is* the harm?"

"The harm is, we can't trust her, AND we're in a hurry," TJ replied in a low voice, grabbing Dean's arm and shaking it. "Do you remember why we're here? Try. We need to get to the Dragon Head, like, now."

They walked off down the street, Dora in front, the Circle inside the light ring. Lady G walked right beside them. The Circle picked up speed and skimmed along the ground. Lady G kept pace with no trouble in her high heels. After a few blocks of rapid travel, she stopped them with a wave of her hand and motioned down a side street. Despite their intention to do otherwise, they made the turn and followed her as if magnetized, coming to a heavy metal door in the side of a building. Lady G tapped an unbroken nail on the door. It swung open, revealing a short hallway leading to some descending stairs. From the floor below, the boom of bass and drums pounded deep inside.

She turned to them with a big smile. "Welcome to Oblivion. Step this way." Lady G waved her hand at the doorway of Club Oblivion as if she was inviting them to a garden party.

The Circle stared into the doorway with varying degrees of suspicion. "Are you out of your mind?" Audrey's voice rose. "We're not going in there with you."

Willet covered her ears and beat a retreat in the opposite direction to escape the ear-pounding music. The light ring shattered without the full Circle.

Dean said, "Music. It sounds good." He launched himself through the doorway and disappeared down the dark flight of stairs.

That left TJ and Audrey standing at the door with Dora, eye to eye with Lady G, who smiled her toothy smile. "My, my, your sparkly ring is gone. What will happen to you now?"

Dora rose to her feet. A low growl curdled deep in her throat, and her curled lips exposed canines even more deadly than her growl. Lady G backed into the doorway.

TJ put an arm around Audrey. "I'll go get him. You take care of Will. Stay away from this door and keep Dora with you. I'll be as quick as I can."

With that, he pushed through the doorway past Lady G, who laughed as if someone had told a hilarious joke. She turned her back on Audrey and slammed the door shut.

Audrey and Dora hurried back up the street and found Willet around the corner, crouched on the ground against the side of the building with her hands pressed to her ears. "You have to stay with Dora and me, Will," Audrey said when she caught up to her sister. "She's our best protection now."

Willet dropped her hands from her ears. "I tried to manage the noise, but it's hard to control my ear drums with so much low vibration. I can't go in there, no way."

"Of course, you can't. I won't either." Audrey pulled Willet up to standing. "Dean has lost his mind. Who knows what's going on in that place?"

"Where is Thomas? Why isn't he with you?"

"TJ went in after him. We need to wait here and hope he can convince Dean to come out."

Willet and Audrey peeked around the corner from the edge of the building, hoping to see TJ and Dean emerge from the club. Dora stood close beside them, her eyes scanning their surroundings.

"Can you spin a ring around just the two of us?" Willet said. "That would make me feel better."

Audrey tried a ring. It sputtered and died. "Honestly, I'm spent. I've kept the rings going since we left the Park. I've got no spin left. Without the full Circle, I can't get anything going. Maybe if I rest a while, I can try again."

"No ring, no Circle. I have a bad feeling, Auddie."

"You and me both, hon."

*****

Dean followed the siren song of screaming guitars and pounding drums down the stairway to the club floor. The thrum of the bass pulsed in his feet and pounded against his chest. He wanted to get closer, close enough to feel it in every muscle. He entered the main room where a four-piece rock band played on a stage. The music coursed through his blood with an inexplicable feeling of power that set his teeth on edge. The beat lifted him to that level of exaltation that had made him want to be a rock musician since he first heard Led Zeppelin on his father's CDs.

A singer fronted the band with harmonica in hand and a cascade of curly black hair flopping around his face. He howled and grimaced as he sang and then wailed on the harmonica. Dean didn't care if the lyrics were good or if there was a melody. Everything he felt about the ecstatic energy of rock and roll was conveyed in the pounding beats and the urgent squeal of that harmonica. It was so raw, so beautiful. He felt ready to jump out of his skin. He had to pound on some drums soon, or he'd punch his fists into a wall. The big set of black and silver chrome Ludwig drums and the Zildjian cymbals on stage called to him. He itched to be up there, in the flow of the music. A woman's voice whispered in his head. "Go ahead. Play the drums. Sing. You know you want to. Stay with me, and you will always have a band and a stage." *Yeah, I could stay here, just play music. Why not?*

*****

TJ felt his way down the dark stairs leading into the club. The stone walls felt cold and clammy, the stairs slippery. Music echoed off the walls. His eyes adjusted to the very low light. When he reached the bottom step, he walked into a sharp left turn and entered the main room. After the clammy darkness of the stairs, this room felt hot, bright and deafening.

On stage, three guitars, a singer and a drummer thrashed heavy metal. The singer was a screamer, not his favorite type. If there were lyrics, they were incomprehensible. Behind the band, fire shot up from a row of small jets, reflecting light off the cymbals and chrome rims of the drums. Smoke from the jets made TJ's eyes water, and the bass hit his chest so hard he thought his breastbone might crack.

The floor in front of the stage was filled with dancers, their auras shimmering silver, black, gray, bronze, and deep red. Undulating bodies could barely be distinguished, except for one. Dean stood in a glow of orange-gold right in front of the stage, his eyes fixed on the band. His hands made rapid drumming motions and fist pumps.

That idiot! TJ elbowed his way to the stage and stood next to Dean. "We have to leave!" he yelled in Dean's ear. "The ladies are outside by themselves."

Dean looked at TJ like he didn't recognize him. "I'm going on stage."

"What? No you're not."

"I'm the headline drummer. Lady G said so. I'm going to tear this place apart." With that, Dean leaped onto the stage ad ran to the drummer, grabbed the sticks out of his hands and pushed the guy off his seat, and then sat down and started banging. There was a momentary lull as the beat faltered, but Dean started swinging the sticks, clobbering the drumheads and spanking the high hats. People started dancing again, hands in the air, and the place exploded with a visceral energy both violent and sexual. The singer stepped to the front of the stage and launched into a vocal.

TJ didn't recognize the tune, but it sure did cook. The bass and drums worked together like a fine-tuned engine, weaving hypnotic patterns that grabbed him by the chest and wouldn't let go. He was mesmerized and couldn't help moving to the music. Behind the massive kit, Dean was lost to his own beat. TJ could see it in his eyes, and it made him stop moving. How was he going to get an out-of-control drummer intoxicated by adrenaline and a driving beat off the stage and out of the club? The answer was actually simple when he thought about it. He owned Club TJ in West Hollywood for several years before Red Souls burned it to the ground. He knew how to distract a crowd from the thrall of a band. Start a brawl.

He whirled around and punched hard into a dark gray aura right behind him, aiming for what he thought might be the head. *Sorry, whoever you are.* His hand connected with a face, and he felt the crunch of bone under his knuckles. *Hope that wasn't a woman.* Whoever it was tumbled backward, knocking into other aura-shrouded bodies. Pushing broke out on the dance floor, followed by fighting and yelling, degenerating into the perfect brawl. Someone grabbed TJ's shirt and tried to drag him to the floor. He threw an upper cut that hit a chin and felt teeth crack inside it. Then he leaped onto the stage. He searched for cables to pull and stop the sound. Oddly, none of the guitars were connected to amps or power supplies, so he went up to the bass player and ripped the bass guitar out of his hands with a sharp pull. The guitar strap snapped. *Really sorry buddy.* TJ threw the guitar out into the crowd, and the bass player launched himself after it. The crowd scrambled to get out of the way. The guitar hit the ground and the musician landed on top of it. Dean's drumming faltered when the bass went silent.

TJ went to the drums and yanked Dean off his stool, yelling in his ear. "We need to get out of here!" Dean looked dazed. TJ shook him and looked in his eyes. "It's me. It's TJ. Let's book before we're trapped here." He grabbed Dean's elbow, put an arm around his shoulders, and pulled him to the side of the stage. They stumbled down a short set of wooden steps and ran right into Lady G.

"Where do you think you're going?" she hissed. "You have a show to do." She drew close to Dean, rubbed her hands over his chest with voracious eyes like she wanted to devour him.

TJ felt Dean's body shiver through his clothes. He pushed her hands away. "Keep your hooks off him, woman. We're leaving."

Georgina wrapped her arms around Dean's neck and licked her lips. Her long canines sprang out over her upper lip. It looked like she was leaning in to bite him. TJ shoved her away hard with his forearm. She stumbled back several steps before falling and then sprung into a crouch and started scrambling forward on all fours, a disturbing sight made more so when her body morphed fluidly into a large black and brown spider with six legs and Lady G's head, which was way too big for the body. She moved toward them fast with a frenzied look in her eyes. When she got to Dean, she raised her long front legs onto him as if to climb up his body.

TJ kicked his foot at the she-spider's gut and sent her sliding backwards again. Her angry screeches were ear-piercing. He dragged Dean into the hallway, and Dean began to stumble ahead on his own. They ran up the stone steps taking them two at a time. It was dark at the top. They reached the door, and TJ jammed his shoulder against it. The door wouldn't budge. He felt for the handle and turned it. The door creaked open. *Halleluiah, it's not locked.* The two men burst out to the sidewalk, slammed the door shut and leaned their shoulders against it, breath heaving. It took a moment before they noticed the cloud of snow-white light glowing in front of them against the surrounding gloom.

In the center of the light stood Gem in her long purple skirt and white peasant blouse with ruffled neckline. Her brown eyes flashed, and her toe tapped with impatience. Smoke rode on her breath like dry ice, and her icicle stare pointed right at them. "What kind of warrior behavior is this?" she asked. Her slow, enunciated words were colder than her eyes.

To be fair, Dean and TJ had never called themselves warriors. That was Gem's term. They were sweaty and disheveled, and TJ's knuckles were bleeding. Maybe that could be construed as warrior-like in some circles, but not the kind of warrior the Guardian was looking for. She expected dedicated, upright fighters defending truth, justice and the Way of Light. TJ and Dean could barely meet her gaze.

"Well?" she demanded. "Where are the sisters?"

"Sorry, Gem," Dean muttered. "I wanted to hear the music. TJ had to come to get me. It's totally my fault. Don't know what got into me. Glad you're back, by the way."

Gem huffed. "So, we are missing a Listener *and* a Ring Thrower. How is this mission to be accomplished?"

"We'll find them," Dean said. "They wouldn't have gone far."

"Will and Audrey are safe with Dora, I'm sure," TJ added.

Snarls and screeches reached them from around the corner, laced with cries from familiar female voices. So much for safety. Gem took off in the direction of the sounds with TJ and Dean close behind her.

Chapter 4

Bart drove as fast as he could without tipping the wobbly wooden enclosure full of crystal bags off the back of his truck. Nick and Jain held on to shoulder straps to keep from banging into each other. Jain suggested shortcuts through Little Armenia and Thai Town to get to Griffith Park more quickly. Bart hesitated to take the suggestions at first but found Jain was right. They did speed up the journey. They soon approached the Park entrance. Bart slowed and let the truck climb the long entry road at a pace it could handle.

When they reached the Observatory area, they found – nothing. No one was there, just a few cars, seemingly abandoned. They got out and walked to the front doors of the Observatory building. They were locked. They walked around to the back balcony. There, far below the balcony, the dragon headed statue stood at the foot of the mesa, looking much the worse for wear after melting and cooling. Its huge dragon head hung to the side and the whole body was lopsided - the stuff of storybook nightmares.

"Wow," Nick marveled. "It marched all the way here and then stopped. Maybe the military guys melted it."

Bart knew it wasn't the military. "Dean and Audrey did this. It's what they do, why they had to come to Griffith Park, I guess."

Jain walked from one end of the balcony to the other, looking over the ledge for signs of life. "Your friends got some kind of fire power," he said. "Must have been a kick-ass fight."

Back at the truck, they saw a man, two women and a boy walking out of the trees from the other side of the central mall. "We have to talk to them." Bart said. Bart and company went over to meet the small group. "We're looking for our friends," Bart said. "They were supposed to be here. Did you see a man and woman, or maybe two men and two women together? I'd like to know what happened to them or where they went." He was almost embarrassed to say it, but he had to. "One woman may have had a green glow about her…"

The dark-haired man with a beard answered them. "What do you want to know?" He spoke in a friendly voice with a distinct accent, but his dark eyes were sharp.
"About the statue," Bart said. "Do you know what happened to it?"

"We know," the man replied. "The Circle did its work and moved on."

"Where did they go?"

"Downtown," said the man.

The boy held the hand of the red-haired woman. "I want to find Mr. Tom," he said. He looked up at the woman. "I should be with him, Mom. He needs me."

The red-haired woman put an arm around the boy's shoulders. "Jonah, you need to stay right here with Arhat and me, where you'll be safe."

The boy wriggled out of her embrace. "I'm not a baby. I can help." He stalked away toward the trees.
The other woman with them had a long tail of brown hair. She stood almost six feet tall, dressed in gray cargo pants and a maroon jacket. Her brown eyes gleamed with steady light. "What is your interest in the Circle?" Her voice had a bell tone to it.

Bart thought for a minute. Why *did* he want to find them? "Well, they're friends of mine, Dean and Audrey. Willet too. I have a truck load of crystal chips they might want. Dean says it's good in a fight against, uh, weird stuff that tries to kill you. That's what the Circle does, right? Fight weird stuff that shouldn't exist..." He wasn't sure if he had said too much.

Nick and Jain turned on Bart and exclaimed almost in unison.

"You have crystal in your truck? Why didn't you tell us? We showed you ours!"

Bart shrugged. "Sorry, I didn't really know you guys. Now we all know."

The man scratched his chin through his beard. "If your crystal can give the Circle an advantage in their fight, then it is good you bring it to them."

"What is the fight, exactly?" Bart asked.

"They fight an ancient evil, not easily defeated."

Dean had explained about Jat. Bart didn't fully understand who Jat the Deceiver was, but he had seen the damage he could do. Jat's crystal attack pushed Bart's house down a cliff and into a ravine, a total loss. The Wall of Unknowing had tried to swallow him whole when he got too close to it. An ancient evil indeed. "Do you know where in downtown they went?" he said.

"The biggest building, called the Dragon Head. It is the center of the negative force gripping the city. You will find them there."

"That's where the statue came from," Jain said, getting agitated. "I saw it step off the top of that building. Its legs went all the way down to the street, a mile long. It was impossible. That place is cursed!"

"Nevertheless, the building must be faced and defeated," said the man. "Like all our fears."
Bart was unsure how to respond. He had a feeling the man knew much more than he was saying. "I'm Bart. This is Nick and Jain."

The man nodded. "I am Arhat Anselmi."

There was something familiar about Arhat, a certain light in his eyes that Bart had seen before. "Do you know Gem?"

Arhat smiled. "Yes. I serve as a Teacher for the Circle of Augustus. For centuries, it has been my honor to serve all Guardians in this capacity."

That explained his understanding of the situation. "Please, Arhat. Anything you can tell us would be helpful. We have to find them and deliver the crystal."

Arhat's eyes met Bart's with an unflinching stare. "The building must be reduced to dust. It is the only way to free the city."

"It's a really big building," Jain said. "How they gonna do that?"

"The Circle has the power of Spirit behind it. The crystal will help."

"Is there anything else we should do, besides deliver the crystal?" Bart asked. "Anything we should look out for?"

"Keep the light in your heart. Distrust what you see. Control your emotions and be ready to provide your full strength when called upon." Arhat continued his sharp, appraising stare to make sure Bart had understood the word.

Heavy advice from someone they just met. Bart thanked Arhat and motioned Nick and Jain to get in the truck. "Dean and Audrey have a long lead on us. We want to get there before a fight starts."

*****

Around the corner from Club Oblivion, a giant leathery-winged raptor dropped from the sky like a bomber and aimed straight for Willet and Audrey. The sisters pressed themselves against the side of the building, hiding behind Dora with their arms covering their heads. The raptor's gaping jaws opened wide as it dove down, jagged teeth trying to grab a mouth full of the sisters. Dora jumped up to meet the raptor and knocked it away with her head. She blasted the raptor with fire, scorching its belly and face. The wide-winged predator gave a furious screech and flew up in a spiral, then readied for another plunge. Dora stood ready to meet the attack.

Gem, Dean and TJ rounded the corner in time to see Dora's body expand to the size of a small horse. The Hound snorted fire and leaped into the path of the raptor, intercepting it in mid-swoop, then plunged her canines into its leg. The raptor struggled to free itself, tried to fly up and away, but Dora held it fast. The raptor flapped its wings frantically and ripped at the back of Dora's neck with teeth and claws, raking long bloody gashes through her flesh. Dora held on. The cement pavement turned to liquid, and a pit opened below her feet belching smoke and flames. Dora dragged the raptor down, bringing it closer to the mouth of the pit even as blood streamed down her neck. The raptor squirmed and twisted and tried to rise into the air.

"Dora! Look out!" Gem exclaimed. The Guardian gathered a Freezing Breath and her lungs filled with cold water. She blew the icy liquid into her hands and formed a long icicle with a sharp point between her palms, then pressed the icicle to her shoulder and launched it at the raptor like a shot putter. The strength and precision of the throw made both TJ and Dean gasp in shock.

The spear pierced the raptor's chest and plunged all the way through its back. The raptor spun in the air like a chicken on a spit, howling, unable to do anything to dislodge the spear.

The voice of Jat the Deceiver emerged from the jaws of the raptor. "It is too late, Guardian. Your defenses are feeble." The derision in his voice curdled the air. "This war will be won on my terms."

"You are skewered, Deceiver," Gem cried. "Finish him, Dora."

The body of the raptor twisted backward. It tried to sink claws and teeth into Dora's flank, but Dora's teeth were still embedded in the raptor's leg. She jumped into the smoking pit, dragging the raptor with her. With a sharp toss of her head, she flung the body of the raptor deep down into the pit and jumped out. The pit shriveled and disappeared, leaving nothing but smooth pavement. The big dog hung her head, panting, gulping air, and gradually returned to her normal size. She collapsed onto her belly, head on her paws, and whined softly. Shivering tremors rolled through her body.

Gem ran to her and dropped to her knees beside her Hound, kissed the top of Dora's head and examined the vicious bites on her neck. "Oh, my dear brave girl, you are wounded." Gem blew a cold breath spangled with ice crystals over the wounds. The bloody gashes steamed.

The sisters knelt beside Dora and gently stroked her back. They would not be comforted by TJ and Dean. Their concern was all for Dora. "The wounds look bad, Gem," Willet said, still shaking. "She'll be alright, won't she?"

"They went at it tooth and claw," Audrey added, her voice trembling. "Dora was bleeding so badly, I thought she might lose the fight. You got here just in time, or that big bird would have carried one of us away."

Gem didn't take her eyes off Dora. "Dora is invincible when she fights in the Underworld, but when she is in a physical body, she is vulnerable to the Deceiver's venom." Gem blew cold breaths on the raw wounds to reduce the inflammation. "She accepts that risk to fight by my side."

"You can heal her, right?" Willet said. "She won't die, will she?"

"I can heal the surface wounds, but the Deceiver's poison spreads in her body. Dora herself must burn through it. The pain is terrible." Gem stroked her hand over Dora's head. "You remember the burn on your skin when Jat sprayed us with the Venom of Despair. It is incapacitating to most Souls. The Hound of Hell can overcome it, but it will take much energy. I pray she still has enough." Gem sat back on her heels, took a deep breath, and laid her hand on Dora's back. "Guardian and Hound shall not be separated if I have anything to do about it, not by Jat and not by death. This I vow."

Dean dropped to the ground beside Dora. "I'm sorry," he said. "I should never have left you guys. This wouldn't have happened." No one argued.

Red gashes on Dora's neck lost their angry, inflamed look, but tremors continued to shake her like a fever. Tight spasms cramped in her neck and back. She rolled on her side, struggling for breath, and began to convulse. Heat rose from her body in visible waves, so hot it could be felt by everyone near her.

Gem blew a layer of wet, heavy snow from head to tail over the shuddering black dog. "I have never seen her like this." She blew cool air softly across the big dog's head and ears. "Please do not leave us. Do not leave *me*."

The Circle surrounded Dora and Gem in helpless silence, stricken with worry. They sang a soft 'HU' chant. Dora's ragged breathing sounded as if it would tear her lungs apart. How much longer could she go on like this? The tremors subsided. Dora took a deep breath and closed her eyes. She wasn't breathing. Agonizing seconds passed. It seemed the breath of life had left her body for good.

"No Dora, no," Gem whispered. She laid her head on Dora's side, refusing to let the big dog go, waiting for the rise of the next breath. It didn't come, it still didn't come. An eternity of waiting. Surely Dora couldn't live without breathing for this long. And then a breath rose. Dora's ribs expanded and she heaved a bit sigh. Her breathing settled into a shallow rhythm. It sounded almost normal. Sighs of relief rose from all of them. Willet and Audrey hugged each other.

Audrey stood up and turned on Dean. She was not in a forgiving frame of mind. "You left us in a place like this? I can't believe you left us. You're a selfish dope!" She paced up the sidewalk and back clenching and unclenching her fists. She looked like she was ready to throw a punch. Dean didn't try to defend himself. He just hung his head.

"Blaming each other will get us nowhere," Gem said, rising to her feet. "I do not want Dora troubled by our conflicts. She needs her strength to heal."

"There was a screw up, admittedly," TJ offered. "We need to move past it."

"Move past it?" Audrey jeered at TJ. "We almost got ripped apart by a prehistoric animal. Dora almost died. While you two were doing god knows what with that witch. And suddenly you're a peacemaker? You didn't believe in any of this as I recall!"

"That's ancient history, Ms. Perfect," TJ said. "Like *you* pretending to be the leader of this group."

"Auddie, calm down," Willet said. "You're making things worse."

"I get it. You're angry," Dean said. "You have a right to be. I don't know what came over me. It was like hypnosis or something. I just wanted to hear the music."

Audrey turned on him. "The witch hypnotized you. Is that what you're saying?"

The volume of Dean's voice rose to match Audrey's. "It had nothing to do with her! She didn't interest me in the least. It was the music."

"That is the most selfish excuse I've ever heard. It's always something with you. 'Audrey, I was infected by Red Souls,' She mimicked his voice. 'Audrey, I was hypnotized by a witch. Audrey, we'll have our time together when this is over.' You're full of it."

"And you're a sanctimonious pain in the ass!" Dean shouted. Audrey walked away and he watched her go. "Will, your sister is wearing out my last nerve."

Retorts flew fast between them. "Like you have room to talk." "Yeah, you're no help." "You're blaming this on *me*? You're an idiot!" "Look who's talking!"

Gem watched the escalating exchange of vitriol with a raised brow and a glint of exasperation in her eyes. The Guardian had ways of dealing with out-of-control negativity, and she chose to apply one now. She filled her lungs with cold, pursed her lips and blasted them with a frigid wind strong enough to knock them back a few steps. Icy snow hit them in the face. After a minute, the wind died down. They struggled to regain their balance and shake off the melting ice.

Gem regarded them with a stern expression. "Whatever issues you have with each other, please release them now. You have allowed the illusion of this realm to obscure your good sense. It weakens the unity of the Circle. Dora sent Jat the Deceiver to the Underworld, but he will rise from the pit again before long. We have little time to do what we came here to do. The Dragon Head Building must be brought down before this city falls. There is danger that the forces of Nature will reclaim the land too quickly for us to save it. Any vestige of this civilization will be lost. Do you understand these words?"

The Circle members stood wet and sheepish and responded with glum nods. "Yeah." "Civilization lost." "It's serious." They were shaking off the cold when Willet took a sharp breath. "I hear clicking again." She knew that sound well. "Needles. Those things are back."

Needle Men poured out of windows, down the sides of buildings and along sidewalks like a deluge of dirty greywater and flooded through the streets. Long shadows came out of gutters and pooled on the sidewalks around them, clicking their needle fingers. Attacks by the Needle Men inside the Wall had left Willet petrified. She had no desire to encounter them again. "Hurry, Auddie," She whispered. "Spin a ring."

Audrey tried to spin a small ring. It sputtered and died on her finger. She tried again and managed to get a small one circling her index finger, then tossed it above her head. It went out in a puff of smoke. Without ring defense, they were easy targets.

"We can perish, or we can behave like the Circle of Augustus," Gem said. "Make a choice."

Audrey spun another ring and threw it above her head, grabbed her sister's hand, and then reached out for Dean with her other hand. He looked at her with questions in his eyes, then wrapped her outstretched hand with his own, then held his other hand out to TJ. TJ took Willet's hand and kissed her fingers. The Circle linked, and the circuit completed. Energy shot through them. Their ring flared out, sizzling and sparking, and encircled them just in time.

The energy ring kept the Needle Men at bay, but did not vanquish them. Needles clicked eagerly at the light's circumference, sliding up to the edge, trying to break through. Gem sprayed the shadows with a barrage of sleet to drive them back. A new flood rushed up to the ring light to take their place. Dora struggled to her feet and managed a breath of fire. Shadows of the Needle Men receded and then swarmed back just as quickly. There seemed no end to them.

Gem twisted a cold breath into a spinning cylinder on her finger, tossed it in the air, and blew into it. The cylinder exploded into a whirlpool of ice and wind and went flying into the mass of the shadows. That got a reaction. The shadows swirled back against buildings and clicked like demented crickets before melting away, but new shadows took their place, more and more of them, like a rising tide lapping at their feet. If the ring light failed, the Circle would be overrun.

"I feel needles poking into my feet," Willet cried out. "How are they getting to us?"

"They're slipping underneath the ring," TJ shouted. "It needs to be thicker!"

Audrey spun rings on all ten fingers and let them drop around the Circle. Gem blew a layer of iced rain over the Circle to reinforce the light rings. The pure white lights sparkled like the rings of Saturn and flared out over many city blocks. It swept over buildings, around corners, through windows and down every hole in the ground, attacking shadows like a disinfectant wherever they lurked. The shadows disappeared. Minutes went by. They waited for the next wave of shadows to attack. This time, they did not return. Everyone let out the breaths they were holding. The light rings dropped, and the ice melted into rain drops. For a few moments, it was blissfully silent.

"The Needle Men are very powerful here," Gem said finally. "It took much energy to disperse them. Remember that and keep your lights on."

"Can we get going?" Audrey said. "I don't think I could spin that many rings again right away."

"There's another fight coming," TJ said, pointing down the street. "I've seen this one before."

A spider the size of a mid-size sedan rounded the corner and scuttled toward them on eight spindly legs, its eyes wild, its hungry palps tapping together, eager for prey. It came on fast.

"That's Lady G," TJ said. "She turns into a spider. I forgot to mention that."

"I've had enough of this bitch," Audrey hissed. "She needs to be exterminated." She found a reserve of energy deep inside herself and readied new rings on her fingers. "I'll squash her like the bug she is." She spun up a particularly hot ring on her right hand and hurled it at the spider. The ring hit the spider in the head. Two more rings hit the thorax with force and sent the spider flipping onto its back, long legs wriggling in the air, unable to right itself. A ring twice the size of the others formed on Audrey's left hand. She got ready to deliver a death blow.

Gem laid a light hand on Audrey's arm. "The spider is disabled. Would you take a life to satisfy a grudge?"

Audrey looked at the squirming spider. "I really, really – despise her, Gem. She and her goons tried to kill us. You're telling me I shouldn't I kill her?"

Gem seemed unmoved by the grievance. "Taking a life is a grave act. It will have an effect on *you*. You must decide if the cost of revenge is worth it."

The form on the ground slowly lost its arachnid features and turned into a skinny black-haired female in a tiger print jumpsuit. Lady G got to her feet, stuck out her tongue at them and laughed, then sauntered away, wiggling her behind. Audrey watched her disappear around the corner. Fury burned in her heart. She felt foolish then, and the ring on her finger snuffed out.

"Revenge serves the Deceiver's purpose," Gem said. "It has distracted you, and now the Circle is left without its ring light. We cannot squander our energy and lose ourselves in petty squabbles. It will be our doom."

Audrey stared at her hands. "Nothing makes sense to me anymore," she said bitterly. "I wanted to protect us. I don't know why I'm in this Circle if I can't do that."

"You know why. Everything we see here is designed to deceive. We' dealing with Jat, are we not? If we allow ourselves to be provoked, then our Light will be lost. It will distract us from the real threat we are meant to defeat."

Dean approached them. "Ladies," he said cautiously. "What are we doing? We need to be gone before the Needle guys come back."

"I don't know if I can do it anymore," Audrey said. "I feel useless."

"Warrior, talk to her, please, before she does something she will regret," Gem said, waving a hand at Audrey. She walked away, leaving Audrey and Dean alone.

Chapter 5

Bart put pedal to metal on the drive from Griffith Park to downtown. He wondered at the fortuitous grace of running into Nick and Jain, men who knew about the crystal, and then finding someone who knew as much about the Circle as Arhat did. Small miracles seemed to follow the Circle. He sped south along Hyperion Avenue, unimpeded by traffic. There was an eerie quiet on the streets of Silver Lake, and it was getting harder to see. In the middle of the day, the light was gray and muddy, and everything looked wavy. He had to slow down. The few people on the streets were wrapped in muted colors that swam around them like diaphanous fabric. Nick and Jain stared out the windows, saying nothing. What was there to say? The city seemed to be under a kind of spell. Or was it a curse? Bart had seen the Wall firsthand. He was betting on the latter.

"What do we do when we get to the building?" Nick asked. "What's the crystal supposed to do? Beside make light."

"The crystal does a lot more than make light," Bart replied. "It consumes pollutants in the air, turns it into energy, and stores the energy like a battery. It can work as a battery, in fact. And it grows. The more stuff it consumes, the more it grows. It's a completely renewable energy source. Most important for us, it repels the murky static that is overtaking this city."

"And we were giving it away!" Jain said and shot a look at Nick. "We're idiots."

"People needed light," Nick said. "We had to give it to them."

"You're a gentleman and a soldier, bro," Jain replied. "I'm a capitalist."

"You need money to be a capitalist."

"I used to have money," Jain's voice rose, "A nice apartment, and a sweet bike with a high-performance engine. Now I got nothin'. Nothin'! And some jerk-ass put a rope around my neck! That's messed up! No one puts a rope around James Jain's neck." His tone was as anguished and frustrated as the look on his face.

Bart barely knew the guy, but he felt his pain. He knew that bereft feeling of losing the place you called home. Anyone with eyes could see things were seriously wrong in L.A. Everything had turned weird colors, people walking around in a daze. *I hope the crystal will help…* Suddenly he had to slam hard on the brakes, sending the truck into a swerve. If they hadn't been wearing belts, they all would have gone through the windshield.

Jain clutched at his shoulder belt. "Jeez, dude, what the hell? You put my neck out of whack!"

The truck slid to a stop sideways. Bart pointed at the street ahead. "Someone put out a welcome mat." A spike strip lay across the road, its wicked metal spikes waiting to pop their tires.

"Maybe it's those military guys trying to ambush us," Jain

said, peering out in all directions. "Can we drive around it?

Nick appraised the strip. "No, it's too long, gotta move it. JJ, give me a hand."

Nick and Jain got out of the truck. Jain picked up one end of the strip and pulled while Nick picked up the other end and pushed. As they dragged the strip to the curb, a line of figures appeared out of nowhere, men with long, dark hair, dark jackets and black jeans. They looked like black shadows in the gloom. The line formed a semi-circle around the truck.

"You messin' with our property," a voice said with an accent. "That's a killing offense."

"What do you want?" Nick said.

"We want what you have," came the reply. The voice, male and Asian, came from the middle of the line. A man stepped forward, held a type of baton in one hand and struck the palm of his other hand with it, over and over. It looked heavy. "What's in the truck?"

"Nothing that would interest you," Jain said.

"We be the judge of that."

Bart climbed out of the truck and joined Nick and Jain in the street. "What seems to be the problem?"

"There's lot of bags in the truck. What's in 'em? A lot of anything usually works for us."

"It's construction debris. Plaster. We're taking it to the dump."

"Then you won't mind tossing a bag our way so we can check it out, a toll for passage through our territory."

There were more guys in the line than could be handled by the three of them. The gang carried weapons. Bart didn't have a gun. He wasn't sure about Nick and Jain, but he was sure that once the Asians saw the crystal inside the bag, glittering like diamonds, they would take every bag. He thought about throwing a bag in the leader's face and getting back in the truck. Nick and Jain seemed street-smart. Maybe they would think on their feet and jump in after him. Bart walked to the back of the truck, climbed up the side of the slatted wooden enclosure and lifted a bag off the top of the pile. Something moved underneath. There was sniffling. The bags started sliding, and a head of brown hair emerged from deep in the pile. It was the boy from Griffith Park, Jonah. He was glowing green as a go-light. "What are you doing in there, kid?" Bart exclaimed.

Jonah stood up, unsteady, and blinked his eyes. "Where are we? Is Mr. Tom here?"

"Get out of there right now," Bart scolded. He unlocked the back hatch and lowered it so the boy could jump to the ground. "You're lucky your brain didn't fry. There's – fumes." It could have been deadly for Jonah to be surrounded by the crystal for so long. Bart had seen what the crystal's energy had done to Audrey, and she was adult size.

"Sha Wa!" said the gang leader. "A little green boy? Why is he green?"

"It's the plaster," Bart said. "It's toxic, like I said. You don't want to be around it."

"Just pass the bag. We'll take the kid too. People will pay to see a green kid."

"This boy needs to return to his mother," Bart said with a stern look at Jonah. "You guys don't look like parental types." There were mutters along the line of dark figures. Weapons appeared in their hands, nunchucks. The leader brandished his baton aggressively and pulled his own set of chuka sticks out of his jacket. "You guys are in no position to argue, so do what I say, or we start splitting heads." He walked toward Bart and Jonah, swinging the sticks and waving the baton. He was grinning a nasty smile with a mouth full of metal teeth and made a grab for Jonah.

Nick kicked the guy in the side of the knee when he got close enough. "No ya don't." The knee buckled.

Jain grabbed him around the neck and pulled the guy to his chest. He pulled a little black gun out of his jacket pocket and pressed the barrel of the gun against the guy's temple. "You know what?" Jain hissed through gritted teeth. "I'm getting sick and tired of threats, so, drop the sticks and tell your buddies to go bye-bye or I'll blow a hole in your skull."

He cocked the trigger. Nunchucks clattered to the ground. "That's better. Now why don't you all get lost before I change my mind and shoot you, just for grins."

A voice emerged from the gloom. "Ok, ok, that's enough. Or *I'll* blow someone's head off." A stocky figure of medium height wrapped in a long black coat and black hood pushed his way through the line of figures and came to a stop a few feet away. He had a semi-automatic weapon strapped over his shoulder. "Let's holster the hardware and talk like civilized people."

"We handle this our way, Zeemer," said the leader still tucked under Jain's arm. "This is our catch."

"There's nothing to be caught here," said the man with the big gun. "You know the rules, Liu-San. Kids are off limits. Sir, let the man go. We can sort this out."

Nick put a hand on Jain's shoulder. "J," he said. "Stand down."

Jain pulled his arm off the guy's neck and pushed him away, then stuffed his own gun back in his pocket. The gang leader shrugged, picked up his sticks, and stomped off, throwing up a finger as he went. He and his cohort faded into the shadows. "He called you a Zeemer?" Nick questioned the man. "Some bogus military guys asked us if *we* were Zeemers. Is it a cult or something?"

The man pushed the black hood back from his face. He was round-faced and balding, with wire rim glasses balanced on his nose. "I'm not *a* Zeemer. I'm *the* Zeemer, 'Zeemer Number One' you might say. Name's Rollie Zeemer. And I know what bogus military you're talking about. They call everybody in my group Zeemerites."

Bart cleared his throat. "We do thank you for your, uh, intervention, Mr. Zeemer, but we have somewhere we need to be, urgently. If you don't mind, we'll be moving on now." He turned toward the truck and started walking. Jonah followed at his heels.

"Whoa there," Rollie Zeemer said, "we need to have a little talk first."

He raised his right fist above his head, and three other men in long black coats with hoods suddenly appeared at his back. They were all strapped with big guns. "We maintain order in these parts," Rollie Zeemer said. "Sort of an unofficial Neighborhood Watch. This is my brother, Edgar, a captain of the LAPD," he said gesturing to the man on his left. Edgar dropped his hood and gave a curt nod and a narrow-eyed glare. He was the same medium height, round and balding like his brother. "That there is Chief Clarence Duggins of the LA Fire Department to my right, and beside him is Major Chuck Tomasek, formerly of the U.S. Marines. The Major served six years in the Middle East." Chief Duggins was a tall black man with threads of silver in his hair and beard. Major Tomasek looked grizzled and hard like something left out in the sun too long. His eyes were ice blue and piercing. They wouldn't miss much. "You can call me Rollie," said Zeemer Number One. "I have some questions." He gestured toward the truck. "Your place or mine?"

"We really don't have time for this."

"I insist."

Bart, Nick, Jain, and Rollie Zeemer gathered at the driver side of Bart's truck for a parley. The Zeemer backup crew of three stood guard a short distance away.

"I'd feel better if you put that gun somewhere out of our faces," Bart said.

"Oh, this?" Rollie replied, shrugging off his big gun and setting it on the ground. "I just use it for visual effect. Guns don't work around here anymore. The mechanisms jam. Don't tell anyone in the Liu gang. They prefer nunchaku so, not sure they've caught on yet. It's like the Middle Ages around here. No guns, no electricity, no comms. The only thing that still works is fire. We use kerosene for everything now. It's not very efficient, and we're running out. People horde it. Pretty soon they'll be burning their furniture if they don't want to be left completely in the dark." Rollie opened his jacket. Burnished gold light shimmered off his face like a cherubic angel. He was barrel-chested and looked strong, a cross between a linebacker and an accountant. "That brings me to the important question. What's in the truck?"

Though Rollie Zeemer had an honest air about him, Bart still didn't want to discuss the contents of the bags. "Construction debris, like I told you."

"Buddy, I know it's not plaster, so don't yank my chain. More importantly, what's with the kid? Why is he traveling around with three grown men? Is he your son?"

"No, he's the son of an acquaintance. I didn't know he was in the truck, honestly. He's a stowaway. We need to take him back where he came from before his mother loses her mind looking for him."

"And when will you be doing that, taking him back?"

"As soon as we drop off this load."

Rollie removed his glasses, carefully wiped the lenses with the hem of the shirt under his coat and then settled them back on the bridge of his nose. "Yeah, so we're back to the load you're hauling. Everything about this situation smells fishy to me, especially the involvement of a minor child. You don't seem like bad guys, so let me put it this way. I got people all around here waiting to take hammers and spikes to your truck. Those are the Zeemerites. Don't make me give 'em the word to rip into the tires. Tell me what's in the bags."

Bart didn't see any other recourse except to level with him and hope he was a person that used his brain for thinking and could understand the big picture. "We're carrying crystal that is needed by a group of people who are trying to save L.A. from the mess it's in. I don't know exactly how they're going to use the stuff, but they need it to bring down a building downtown that is key to this whole twisted situation."

Rollie's eyes blinked several times behind his wire frames. "I'm listening."

"The crystal is powerful," Bart said. "It stores a lot of energy. They'll use the energy to destroy the building. Somehow."

"I've never heard of such a thing."

"Neither had I, and I'm a geologist. I studied samples in the lab and verified its properties. I've run my office electronics using nothing but crystal as an energy source. More to the point, it also exerts a certain power against forces that are, shall we say, not of this world. I've seen it in action. Nothing like it has been seen on earth before now, that I know of."

"Where would you have obtained this crystal?"

"Remember the big wedges of earth that erupted through the ground all over L.A. a month ago? They were full of crystal. The origins of it are *mysterious,* but I got a few chips from a friend before the crystal was incinerated. I seeded a field with the chips and grew acres of it in a few days. It spreads like a weed. These bags are full of crystal chips. When Jonah hid under the bags, he absorbed too much of the energy from the chips. That's why he's green."

Rollie held out a hand to Jonah. "Come here to me, boy. Let me feel your head."

"Are you a doctor?" Bart asked.

"I'm a pharmacist, but I have kids. I know a fever when I feel one."

"I don't recommend you touch him, but your choice."

Bart caught Jonah's eye and pointed toward Rollie. The boy shuffled forward. When Rollie pressed his palm to Jonah's forehead, a visible flash of green current ran up his arm and neck all the way to his head. He fell backward on his behind with a huff. His thinning hair smoked, turned gray, then white, and fell out onto his shoulders like so much wispy straw, leaving the top of his head completely bald. It took him a minute to compose himself. He brushed the burnt hair off his shirt and looked up at Bart. "So, it's like that."

"Yeah. It's like that."

Rollie struggled to his feet. "Packs quite a punch. Can I see some?"

Bart opened the bag he held and tapped a few chips into Rollie's hand. Rollie studied the chips, rolled them around in his palm. They sparkled like moonlight on ice, casting sharp patterns of light against his skin, which began to glow faintly green.

After a long moment, he took a deep breath and said, "What can I do to help?"

Chapter 6

After the confrontation with the spider, Audrey remained distraught, and Dean drew her aside, out of earshot of the others. "Don't say you're useless. You're certainly not useless," he said. "I want to help, but I don't know what to do. You seem mad at me all the time."

"I'm just mad. Every silly little thing annoys me. Anger is eating my brain. I take it out on you because you're on my mind a lot."

Dean drew back and looked in her eyes, those beautiful blue eyes now confused and sad. "I don't mind being on your mind. You're certainly on mine."

A deep sigh shook her shoulders. "It upsets me that you and I got robbed of time that should have been ours. I get mad enough to strangle someone over the slightest thing. That woman was the last straw. I was ready to kill her, Dean. Because I knew I could do it easily. I'm not the peaceful person I used to be, and it scares me."

Dean reached out a hand and stroked her hair, then withdrew it. "We've been fighting for our lives for months. None of us are the same people. Look at Willet. She used to hide in her closet to avoid noise. Now she's the Circle's early warning system, listening on the front lines. TJ was all about money and success. Now, he's rescuing children and acting like a UN diplomat. I barely recognize him."

"Those are good changes. My changes are bad."

"We can't go backwards. We have to be who we are now."

"I've turned into an unhappy, sarcastic, dangerous harpy! I don't want to be that."

"That's not really you, babe. You're the kindest and most level-headed woman I've ever met. Jat is messing with us. He'd like us to self-destruct, you know that. We have to help each other keep a grip."

"That's just it. I don't have any grip left! I'm done with the Circle, and I want to go home."

She felt guilty saying that. Energy drained out of her, and everything around her blurred. A gong rang inside her head, the dull clang of a tolling church bell. Twelve o'clock. *Ow. That hurts.* She pressed her hands to her throbbing temples, felt water dripping on her head and shoulders, and looked up. She was standing in rain. Then she recognized where she was, the street in front of the apartment building in New York City where her family lived when she and Willet were children. The sky was cloudy, and rain pelted her. She looked at her wet clothes and realized she was wearing her gray private school uniform from the sixth grade. Her old book bag hung on her shoulder. It was all so real, so in the moment. She was that school girl again.

The glass doors of the building swung opened and a doorman in a red and black hat and jacket came out. "Miss Audrey," he said, "come out of the rain before you catch cold." He ushered her through the doors into the lobby with big windows and brass light fixtures on wood paneling, just as she remembered it. A man sat in the green stuffed chair next to a window reading a newspaper, and a woman in a suit walked past her, headed for the exit. The lights were dazzling bright, as if she had just walked onto a movie set where a scene was in progress. She wasn't sure if any of these people could actually see her.

She crossed the lobby to the elevators in a state of heightened awareness, taking it all in. She pushed the UP button as she had done so many times, and the doors slid open. Once inside, she pressed '11', the floor of her family's apartment. The elevator started to rise. It was like a dream. When the doors slid open again, there was the old brown door of her apartment right in front of her. She reached for the brass doorknob, turned it, and walked into a room so familiar to her, she knew it by heart. The State of Being there, the impossible reality of it, was incredible.

Her mother's burgundy silk couches and mauve damask chairs with curved legs surrounded the low mahogany table in front of the black and cream marble fireplace. The large mirror in a simple gilt frame hung over the mantel, and the engraved brass bowl graced the table. It was one her mother bought at a Sotheby's auction. 'Understated is best', her mother always said. The room was so understated in its elegance that the family hardly ever used it except during the holidays. Souvenirs from her father's archeological digs and excursions were stored in glass cabinets in the family room, but mother did display a row of carved long boats with figures in them that he had brought back from Sumatra. They were on the mantel next to the family photo of a trip to the dunes, one of the early happy memories before things got difficult.

Audrey wanted to go to the mantel and pick up those familiar objects, feel them in her hands, but voices floated out from the back hallway. It was her parents, arguing. They walked into the living room, still arguing, and didn't react to Audrey standing there. The subject was Willet as usual.

"We're not sending her to a mental institution," her father said. "She's not mental, she's – gifted. How many times do we have to have this conversation?"

"Bill, she hears voices," her mother insisted. "That's schizophrenia. Her headaches incapacitate her. She hides in her room all day with pillows over her head, talking to herself. It's not healthy. She needs more care than we can give her at home. I can't deal with it anymore."

"It always comes around to you, Agnes, what you need, what you can deal with. Willet is our daughter. She needs to be with the people who love her."

"You're away half the time! I'm here every day, giving her meds, coaxing her out of bed, getting her to eat. Do you know she throws up almost every day? I don't know what to do for her!"

"Stop it! She can hear you!" Audrey shouted, but her parents didn't hear or see her.

As soon as she thought of Willet, she was drifting through the apartment walls to the bedroom like a ghost. Her sister was in bed, under the covers, crying. "Will, don't listen to them," Audrey whispered. "I won't let them send you away."

Willet heard her. "My head hurts so bad," she moaned. "I'm going to be sick again. They don't want me, Auddie. I wish I could just die."

Audrey felt desperately upset for her sister. "That's not true, little girl. Dad wants you. Mom is just, I don't know, confused or tired. You and I will leave someday and live somewhere quiet. I promise. No one will send you anywhere."

An old anger at her mother filled Audrey, one she thought she had buried years ago. The anger pulled at her. She lost her sense of being in that place and time as the bedroom dissolved into dots in front of her eyes.

The air seemed to shift and squelch. She got dizzy, and then found herself standing in a long, domed hall lined with gray stone statues on each side standing in alcoves. Tall, robed men held various objects in their hands – books, orbs, spears, and birds. The hall seemed to go on forever into the distance. It made her feel so claustrophobic, she had to get out. She saw a distant door and started to run toward it. Iridescent green-blue lights lit up in the blank eyes of the statues. Their gazes followed her as she ran, and their deep voices sounded like tumbling rocks. 'There is nowhere to go.' A light shone far ahead. She doubled her pace, her breath heaving. A huge spider dropped from the ceiling on a long thread and landed in front of her. She couldn't stop in time and ran right into it, fell backwards and landed hard on her back. The enormous black and brown spider loomed above her, six feet tall. It planted its long fuzzy legs on either side of her body and lowered its head to study her face. Audrey saw the reflection of her own horrified face in its black, glassy eyes. Pincer hooks on its mouth opened and closed, hungry, salivating, poised just above her head.

"I know it's you, Georgina, no matter what you call yourself." Her own voice sounded strange. "I should have decapitated you when I had the chance." She tried to struggle, but realized her arms were pinned to her sides. Sticky threads of a spider web wrapped her so tight she could barely breathe. "I'm dreaming," she gasped. "You're not even here."

A low chuckle came from the spider. "The Stone Lords are dreaming *you*, blondie. Your predicament is entertaining to them. It eases the boredom of their endless vigil. I am here at the behest of Lord Jat. He would like to taste your brain, so I will bring him a juicy piece."

This dream would end badly if something didn't change. Audrey screamed into the face of the spider louder than she'd ever screamed. The spider startled at the battering ram of sound. It raised up on its back legs, antennae waving, preparing to strike. That gong rang again inside Audrey's head. One o'clock. She heard voices, and her chest clenched in panic. She opened her eyes. A ring of worried faces looked down on her, Willet, Dean and TJ, along with a few faces she didn't recognize. "Where am I?" she rasped, struggling to draw breath.

"You're in a coffee shop, Auddie," Willet's quiet voice said. "You got dizzy and passed out. This place was open, and we brought you in, so you could rest for a while."

"I'll bring her some water," said one of the unfamiliar faces.

Audrey took deep breaths to ease the shaking in her body and then raised herself to her elbows and looked around. There were wooden tables, booths and high stools at a coffee bar. The edges of every piece of furniture wavered, blended into whatever was around them. The light was very dim, lit only with a few candles. Large tarps hung over all the windows. Several kerosene camp stoves lined up on the counter, and three baristas tended boiling pots of water on the hissing burners. They drip-brewed cups of espresso, sending the aroma of fresh coffee wafting through the air.

Audrey let her eyes adjust to the dim light. She didn't trust what she saw. "Is this a real place?" she mumbled. "Everything looks fuzzy."

"You're with us," Willet murmured close to her ear. "It's real. What happened to you?"

"I said I wanted to leave the Circle, and all the energy seeped out of me like I was a deflated balloon. I couldn't even stand up, and then I had dreams. More than dreams. They were so real I could swear I was actually there."

"What kind of dreams?"

"I was at home with Mom and Dad, back at our old apartment in Manhattan. You were there too. Mom and Dad were fighting, like they used to. About you. It made me so mad."

"That's in the past, Auddie. It's not real anymore."

"It was real to me, Will. I was in the apartment just like it used to be. Right after that, I was in a hall of statues and that spider woman was on top of me, looking me in the eye. She was about to eat me. I've never been so terrified. I couldn't move, and I screamed until my eyeballs ached. All I hoped for was to die fast."

No one said a word. A waitress returned with a bottled water and two aspirin. Audrey swallowed the pills and drank from the bottle. Then she closed her eyes. "This is their dream, the Stone Lords. We're all in it."

Chapter 7

Jain was not inclined to accept Rollie Zeemer's offer of help. "You were ready to slice our tires a minute ago. Now you want to help us. Why?"

"Not that we couldn't use the help," Bart added quickly.

"I have family, friends and neighbors, a business," said Rollie. "My business can't run without medicines, and nothing is shipping. Crazies in the streets attack anyone showing the least bit of light. For some reason, people in my neighborhood have gathered around me and my family for leadership. They need help to survive in the darkness, and there are no basic services. It's tough to help when I have no idea what's going on, but we formed a sort of impromptu militia to make sure our neighbors weren't terrorized."

"Local action," Nick nodded. "The best defense."

"Well, it's not totally effective," Rollie said. "The Mayor's Guard marched my brother's oldest son off in chains, because light was leaking out of his jacket cuffs. When did that become a crime? We think they took him to the big black building downtown, but no one can get in the place."

"That's where the giant statue came from," Jain said. "Did you see that thing?"

"Yeah, we saw it," Rollie sighed. "What the holy hell. Edgar is frantic and ready to bust heads, so don't tick him off. I just want to know how all this happened, and I want it to stop."

"That's what we all want," Bart said. "That's why we're here."

Rollie nodded. "You guys seem to have more of a clue than anyone else I've talked to, and you have more light in that truck than I've seen in a while. Maybe this is the answer we're looking for."

"It's part of the answer," Bart said, "definitely not the whole answer. What could you do to help us?"

"Like I said, I have people. We know the streets. We know the local gangs, and they know us. We have mechanics, medics, police and fire fighters, ex-military. We could help you get where you need to go. When you get there, we could offer muscle, equipment and engineering know-how. Whatever we got, it's yours if you can end this nightmare."

It was too good an offer to turn down. Bart and Rollie shook on it.

*****

Audrey sat at a table in the coffee shop, a bottle of water in front of her. She stared straight ahead, lost in her own thoughts. Dean sat to one side of her and held her hand. Willet sat on the other side, talking softly.

"This isn't the dream of some statue, Auddie" Willet said. "This is reality."

Whether or not she heard, Audrey gave no response.

Patrons huddled at tables and in booths around the coffee shop, clutching their steaming cups. There were working people and students and street people and a woman with a shopping bag beside her. Their skin glowed in soft shades of blue and green and gold, all trying to maintain their light in a dark world.

In a corner booth in the back, two men and a women wore motorcycle leathers and heavy black boots. Hints of silver glinted off nose rings, earrings, and lip studs in the candlelight. They huddled over their table in mumbled conversation. The tattoos decorating their faces danced on their cheeks as they spoke.

TJ ordered five espresso shots at the coffee bar and brought them to the table. He knocked back two of the shots one after the other. His fingers drummed a steady rhythm on the table. "What are we doing?" he said in a low voice.

"We're having coffee," Dean said, sipping his own shot.

"It's taking too long to get to the Dragon Head Building. We keep getting diverted. Too many things coming at us. Flying birds and Needle Men, spiders." His fingers drummed faster, and his knee shook. "I bet those biker guys know where to get dynamite. I'm gonna ask them." Before anyone could stop him, TJ got up and walked to the back booth.

The biggest biker looked up at TJ and sneered. "What do you want, pretty boy?"

TJ cleared his throat. "Well, I was wondering if you knew where I might buy some dynamite?"

The bikers gave him an incredulous look and laughed. "Why do you think we'd know about dynamite?" the big guy said. His face, neck and bald head were covered with tattoos. "Do we look like criminals?"

"Uh, no, I'm not from around here, and I thought you'd know what's available in the area."

"That's you're problem, asshole. Step away so we can drink our coffee, or I might have to rearrange your face. And tell that woman over there to shut up before I shut her up."

TJ turned around and saw Gem, who was sitting at a table against the wall near the front door with Dora at her feet. She chanted softly under her breath with eyes closed, and soft gold light surrounded her. The room vibrated with the low hum of the chant.

"You mean *that* woman?" TJ said, suppressing a chuckle. "Well, Good luck with that. Sorry I bothered you." He backed away from the biker table and returned to his seat next to Dean. "This should be interesting."

The big guy got up from the back booth and walked over to Gem. "Knock it off, lady," he said with his lip curled. "The singing is annoying." Dora rose to her feet in front of Gem and gave the man a smile that showed all her teeth. The man swung a chain on his belt and hit Dora in the nose. In a fluid motion, Dora's torso swelled in size and her legs grew long enough to match the man's height. She tipped her head forward and looked directly into his eyes with a narrow glare and gave him a long, low, curdling growl.

The man took a big step back and looked around at the other patrons. "This dog's dangerous," he said. "It needs to be put down."

His two friends from the table in back came to his side with chains and knives in hand. A pin-drop could be heard in the shop. One of the bikers made a move forward with a chain, getting too close to Gem. The other biker followed with her chain.

Dora's jaws opened. She huffed a breath of hot steam into their faces. They dropped their weapons and squealed in pain, shielding their scalded faces with their arms. The temperature in the shop rose. The bikers backed up to the front door and exited in a hurry while some patrons slipped out the back way. Dora sneezed and dropped onto her haunches. Gem calmly continued her chant.

"See what I mean?" TJ whispered. "Bikers in a coffee shop? When did bikers start hanging in coffee shops?"

Dean finished his expresso. "That's your take-away from what just happened? Dora sent them running like rabbits. An awesome beat down. Besides, everybody likes coffee."

"We still have no dynamite," TJ muttered.

"Dora is plenty of protection for Gem. Her growl gave me goosebumps."

"I was thinking about us."

"You're really jittery, sweetheart," Willet said. "I'm concerned about you."

"I'm fine," TJ said. He grabbed the espresso shot in front of Audrey and downed it. His knees shook faster. "What I'm saying is, we need to move before we get bogged down in another confrontation."

"Slow down on the caffeine, dude," Dean said. "You're too wired."

"Yeah, well, it's taking forever to get downtown. It makes me nervous. The longer the Dragon Head Building stands, the more nervous I get. I feel like its growing roots. They're crawling into my chest and squeezing my heart. It's getting hard to breathe."

"You're taking your heart meds, right?" Dean said. "You don't want another episode, especially now. I doubt we'd be able to find a good emergency room."

"My heart's fine," TJ growled. "It's this city that's on my nerves. I want to be done and out of here."

"Your horrible experience in that building scarred you," Willet said. "Psychic scars. I can see them. So will Jat, and he can attack that weakness. It may be more dangerous for you to go back there than for the rest of us. You shouldn't go in."

TJ wiped beads of moisture off his upper lip with the back of his hand. "I've had nightmares and cold sweats ever since I was in the laser gauntlet. It left hooks in me, for sure. The Dragon Head is not a safe place for any of us, but at least I know what to expect."

Audrey snapped out of her reverie and sat straighter. "We're being watched," she said to no one in particular.

"What do you mean, Audrey?" Dean asked. "Who's watching us?"

"Can't you feel it?" she replied, looking furtively around the shop. "Someone knows our every move, like a spider on a web, waiting and watching. If we get trapped in the web, we're finished."

TJ eyed Willet's espresso. "Where's the Traveler when we need her?"

"You mean Sonrisa Degas, the spirit being who has traveled through space and time serving the Guardian for over five hundred years? That Traveler?" Willet's sarcasm surprised everyone. It was uncharacteristic of her, but the Traveler was someone they all held in high esteem and awe. "Have some respect," she said. "The Traveler isn't a taxi service. I wouldn't be surprised if Gem is communicating with her right now."

"I meant no disrespect," TJ tried to soothe her, "but I hope Gem is asking for a ride, 'cuz we could use one."

Maria Sonrisa Degas de Megaro was a nun in fifteenth century Spain who experienced frequent visions, lucid dreams and out-of-body travels. When she spoke about these things, others in the Roman Catholic Church thought she was possessed by the devil. The Spanish cardinal of that time was so afraid of her that he ordered her to be buried alive in a casket under the Abbey where she lived to make sure the devil in her did not escape. While so incarcerated, Sonrisa spent hours in contemplation and left her physical body frequently in Soul Travel to go anywhere she wished. She found her way to the Third Plane where Records of Past Lives are stored and mastered the skill of traveling on the Time Track, to the past and into the future. Eventually, she stopped returning to her physical body altogether. Her Mastership of Space and Time Travel brought her into the hierarchy of masters who serve the Guardians of the world. When a past life recall or a glimpse of future consequences was needed to educate a human being, the Traveler was called upon to provide passage. Sonrisa Degas often provided this service to the Guardian of Los Angeles.

Suddenly Willet stood from her chair and faced the front door, stock still and listening. "Stomping feet. Coming this way. We're about to be attacked."

Seconds later, something struck the front door. The door frame sizzled, and the door swung open on smoking hinges. The customers remaining in the shop dove to the floor and hid under tables. A tall man in a black helmet and black padded jumpsuit pushed through the door carrying an odd gun shaped like a trumpet. A dragon insignia stood out on his chest, silver stripes on his arms and silver buckles on his pants. He wore big black boots.

A young woman with a mass of curly red hair had been waiting on tables. She wore a long-sleeve navy blue shirt and pants, but light glowed off the milk-white skin of her face and hands. Everyone called her 'Marva'. She wiped her hands on her apron and walked to the door.

"What do you want?" she said. "You've ruined the door. Who'll pay for this?" The woman looked like a porcelain doll, but she had nerve.

The man pressed a silver button on the side of his helmet. The smoked visor flipped up to show his face. "Silence, woman," he snarled. "I am Commander of the Mayor's Guard, and you show too much light. I could arrest you on the spot, but we are on city business. We suspect fugitives are hiding here. Those individuals must show themselves and surrender to us, or we'll burn this establishment to the ground."

"There are no fugitives here," Marva protested. "What are you talking about?"

TJ gulped down the last espresso. "Matt Gregg calls himself the Mayor of LA.," he mumbled to the others. "If this is his doing, he's definitely looking for us, me in particular. We have to get out of here."

If the Commander of the Mayor's Guard heard these words, he didn't react. "I'll give you ten seconds," he said. "After that, we'll firebomb the place."

Gem and Dora quickly joined Marva at the door. "Perhaps I can help," Gem said. "No need for violence." She slipped between Marva and the Commander and backed the man out the door. Gem followed him out with Dora at her side and closed the door behind her.

Dean stood up. "Gem may want backup. We'll need ring power. Audrey, are you up to this?"

Audrey wobbled as she stood, and Dean took her elbow to steady her. "I'm running on fumes," she said, "but I'll do what I can."

The Circle followed Gem out the front door. A phalanx of militia in black padded jumpsuits with silver stripes down the arms stood in the street holding the same trumpet-shaped guns.

"You cannot detain us," Gem said to the Commander, ever polite, as if she were declining a dinner invitation.

The man bristled. "What you gonna do about it, lady? Huh?"

The face inside the helmet was a man with sharp cheekbones and even sharper brown eyes. He had a short-trimmed salt and pepper beard and mustache framing a mouth twisted in a snarl.

Gem pursed her lips and blew an ice dart at his forehead, so quickly that the man had no time to react. The dart lodged between his eyebrows. His eyes rolled up, knees buckled, and he fell to the ground like a sack of stones. Shouts rose from the militia. In one coordinated motion, they raised their guns and aimed at the front of the coffee shop.

A light ring spun on Audrey's index finger, and she flung it into the air. It expanded and settled around the Circle with a steady hum.

The Mayor's Guard fired a barrage of shots with their trumpet-shaped guns that sounded like popping corn. An invisible force hit the ring, causing it to buckle inward and ripple. A scent of ozone filled the air.

The Circle spread out and fortified its energy ring into a thick whirling disc that deflected the next round of shots.

The shooters staggered on their heels as the shots ricocheted back and hit them. Guns dropped out of their hands, and they froze where they stood.

The gun fire made Willet wince. "What are those guns firing?" she asked. "I don't see sparks or smoke, but I sure feel it in my ears."

"Some kind of pressure wave with lots of energy behind it," Dean said. "See what it did to those shooters? They're immobilized."

Gem crouched beside the downed commander and picked up the gun lying beside him. She plucked the ice dart from between his eyes and rubbed his cheek with it. "Hear me, please," she said. "Tell me what you are shooting from these guns."

The man's eyes popped open. He shook his head to clear his brain and then coughed. "Why should I tell you?"

"You are firing at my Circle. I will not allow that."

The man just laughed.

Gem stood up, leveled the weapon under her right arm and aimed it squarely at his face. "I will shoot you with this thing unless you tell me what it does, and I will not miss."

The sight of the gun barrel pointed at him changed the man's mind and his demeanor. "I'd rather you didn't."

"Why not?" Gem said. "What does the gun do?"

"It shoots a current that short-circuits the brain. Makes a person docile, easier to manage. Gets rid of any pesky rebellious thoughts, as the mayor says, long enough for us to take a criminal into custody. Genius, really. Mayor Gregg invented it." The man had a satisfied smile on his face.

"I doubt that very much," Gem said. A weapon that nullifies free will had Jat's name all over it. She wondered if the commander had been hit with a shot himself. He seemed so amenable to turning other people into sheep. "What about the soldiers that were hit by the gun fire?"

"Our vests absorb most of the current," the man said. "They're blanked out, but they'll snap back quicker than someone without a vest."

Gem looked with disdain at the weapon in her hand. "This should not exist. The Circle will destroy them. We will take the vests to protect ourselves if we encounter other such weapons."

"Doesn't that violate a law?" the man asked with a smirk of the lips. "Something about stealing?"

"Self-defense is its own law," Gem replied without a trace of humor.

The man made a quick grab at Gem's foot, trying to trip her. Gem fired the gun at his face. The man's eyes blanked, and his mouth went slack. "Now remove your vest," she said. He immediately took it off.

*****

Bart had to decide what to do about Jonah the stowaway. The boy's skin still had a green tinge from the crystal, but there was no time to take him all the way back to Griffith Park to his mother. To avoid touching him and getting shocked, Nick and Jain decided to ride with Rollie Zeemer in his vehicle while Jonah sat in the truck with Bart, at the far end of the front seat.

With seating arrangements settled, Bart's truck rolled off toward downtown, this time with an escort of three trucks and Rollie Zeemer's car flanking him. The trucks were loaded with tools and supplies. Bart felt more confident than before that they would reach the Dragon Head Building with a full load of crystal intact. He turned his attention to Jonah. "How do you know Dean and Audrey and their friends, huh?"

"I know Mr. Tom," said Jonah. "He saved me from a weird circus in that big building, and from a guy who made metal fly at us. He saved my mom too. I feel safer when I'm with him. Mom can't protect me like he does."

Weird circus? Flying metal? Prolonged exposure to the crystal might have addled the boy's brain. Bart met TJ only a couple of times, including the time he had to pull TJ's unconscious body out of an SUV and deposited it in a bed at Pine Siskin House. Never really had a conversation with the man, but he didn't seem like the type to put himself out for others. "This isn't a safe place for you, Jonah," Bart said. "TJ has a big job to do. It's dangerous. He can't look after you right now."

"But I can help him. He needs me."

"It would help him to know you're safe, like you were with your mother and Arhat. If he knew you were here, he'd worry." But what could be done? The kid was here. "How old are you, Jonah?" Bart asked.

"Thirteen," Jonah said, raising a defiant chin.

No way Jonah was thirteen. Bart guessed eleven, max, but the boy was certainly growing into a teenage body. His jeans were too short by an inch, and he was almost busting out of his Lakers T-shirt. His tousled brown hair was matted, like he'd been sleeping on the ground.

"So, what do you think you could do to help?"

"I'll shock anybody who tries to hurt him." Jonah raised his hands and wiggled his fingers. The green glow was almost faded. Soon he would have no juice left. When Bart brought up this fact, Jonah said, "I'll get in the back of the truck and lay on the bags. It felt kinda good before. I'll do it again."

Bart shook his head. "Sorry, can't let you do that. Too much exposure is probably bad for your health. Besides, TJ and his friends will need what's in the bags to fight their fight. You don't want to use up their mojo, do you?"

Jonah went silent again. A crease bunched between his eyes, and his mouth worked as if he were chewing on the information, conflicted between what Mr. Tom needed and what Jonah wanted to do to help him. Bart hoped it would keep his thoughts off the crystal.

It got darker the closer they got to downtown. Static distorted the air and lightning stabbed through the darkness. Shadows of black, silver and gray glinted off anything made of metal. It was hard to see anything clearly. He slowed the truck to a crawl and rolled down the window. *Where are the trucks that were following me?* He stopped, climbed out and made his way to the back of the truck. The atmosphere felt as thick and sluggish as a summer storm. Through the gloom, he spotted the other trucks stopped along the street with hoods up, men looking into the engines. Everyone seemed to be broken down.

He looked back at his own truck. It shimmered with iridescent green light. Crystal in the truck bed glowed through the weave of the burlap bags and lit up the sides. Green light circled the hub caps in thin currents. He crouched to look underneath the chassis. A current of light flowed along the axles into the tires and along the drive train and drive shaft into the engine. He went to the front of the truck and raised the hood. The engine was bathed in the same green light. If his truck still moved when others couldn't, it must be crystal energy that powered it. Bart counted on the support of Rollie's team to help him get to the Dragon Head Building. Now he had to rescue *them*. There was Jonah to think about too. He and the boy would be on their own without backup. He called out to Rollie and soon got an answering call.

Rollie, Nick, and Jain came into view, struggling up the street as if they were pushing though a wind tunnel. The heavy atmosphere seemed to resist their movement. The men approached the green beacon of the truck with arms outstretched, throwing all their strength forward. When they finally reached it, they bent over, hands on knees, to catch their breath.

"I wasn't sure I'd make it," Jain gasped. "It felt like running in mud."

"Me too," Nick said. "I thought I was going to fall backwards."

Rollie sat down beside the truck and leaned against a wheel. "Light. It feels good."

"Did your car break down?" Bart asked.

"All of a sudden, it just rolled to a stop," Rollie said. "Weirdest thing. Happened to all three of the trucks too."

"We can't stay here, Rollie. We have to keep going."

Rollie closed his eyes for a moment and leaned his head back against the big glowing hubcap behind him. "We could ditch the car and ride with you, I guess, if your truck still runs."

"My truck runs fine, but where will everyone sit? All I've got is the front seat."

"I can ride in the back, with the crystal bags," Rollie said.

Bart's eyebrows shot up. "Sure you want to do that? You'll get really juiced. It could be, uh, unhealthy for you…at your age…"

He got a sideways glare from Zeemer Number One. "What do I look like, Methuselah? I'll take the chance," Rollie said. "I wouldn't mind delivering a shock to a few goons if I see them. I need to find my nephew and bring him back to his father."

"I want juice too," Jain added. "I'll make them fry for the rope they put on me. Nick, you're in the front. It's better that way. You shouldn't over-amp yourself, with your nerves and all."

"My nerves are fine, J," Nick said. "I don't need baby-sitting. And what about the kid? If he's radioactive, I shouldn't be close to him, right?"

"Jonah's charge has run down," said Bart. "That's what happens. It's not permanent."

"Even better." Rollie got to his feet. "I'm ready to power up."

"What about the trucks?" Bart said. "We need what's in them, and we can't just leave the people here."

"Well," Rollie said, scratching his chin. "Let's give the drivers some crystal, see if they can get their rides running. It seems to work for you. What about that?"

Bart hesitated to part with even one more bag of the precious cargo, but if it was necessary to keep the caravan together, he'd do it. He climbed up the side of the truck, grabbed a bag of crystal off the top of the pile, and threw it down to Rollie. "Here. Give pieces of the crystal to the drivers. Tell 'em to put chips near the engines. Some on the floorboard might help, and the truck beds too. And bring back what you don't use."

After the crystal was distributed, Rollie and Jain jumped into the back of the truck to sit atop the bags of crystal. Bart had serious misgivings about the seating arrangements, but they were grown men making their own decisions. Fortunately, the rest of the trucks in the caravan managed to get their engines running with the help of the chips. They all got back in line behind Bart's truck. With their crystal lights glowing, the caravan looked like a Parade of Lights float at Disneyland. They also had better visibility, but it was still tough driving. Long thin cracks in the concrete leaked smoke and sparks all the way down Sunset Boulevard. Asphalt was melted, sidewalks sagged, and curbs were broken apart. People huddled in shop doorways, unable to find a safe place to walk. It looked like the city would collapse under its own weight. Maybe that was the 'fall into the Underworld' Dean talked about. Bart hadn't taken it seriously until now. Seeing it firsthand inspired a new sense of urgency. If they didn't bring the crystal to where it was needed, and if Dean and company were not there to do something useful with it, they might all fall into a deep hole. He jammed harder on the gas, hoping the caravan could keep up.

Jonah stared out the window. What he saw clearly scared him. He looked away and closed his eyes.

Nick, who sat between Jonah and Bart, put out a hand and gave a light pat to the boy's knee, still wary of being shocked. "Don't worry, boy," Nick said, "we'll take care of it. You'll see."

Jonah did not seem convinced. "We need Mr. Tom," he said. "He knows about this stuff. When will we see him?"

Bart couldn't lie to the boy, but he felt at a loss to offer any concrete encouragement. "Jonah, we don't know where TJ is, or where he'll be when we get downtown. It may be very dangerous." That was appropriately vague, but Bart had to make sure Jonah understood the risk. "You will stay in the truck. Do not leave it. Do you understand?" Jonah blinked his troubled brown eyes at Bart and nodded. Bart hoped that meant actual acceptance of the command, but he couldn't be sure. He had little experience with pre-teens. "You won't be alone. Nick will stay with you, right Nick?"

"What?" Nick protested. "I gotta help JJ! He can't be out there without me. He'll need backup."

"What is it with you and Jain? It's like you're joined at the hip."

"Me and J been friends since we were ten. We're brothers and we stick together, look after each other. That's the way it is."

"OK." Bart nodded. "I respect that."

"Nobody gets left behind, that's the code. Especially these days."

"I get it. So, how about this - *I* keep an eye on Jain while we figure out what to do with the crystal, and *you* stay with Jonah. He needs protection. You're trained military. I need your help."

"I don't need protection!" Jonah exclaimed.

"Yes, ya do," Bart said. "See what I'm up against, Nick?"

Nick shrugged. "I'll keep an eye on the kid, sure. But JJ's a street fighter. He never admits he's in over his head. Who knows what he'll do with all that green energy? If I see him struggling, I'm goin' in to help him."

"Fair enough." Bart turned off Sunset Boulevard and went south on Glendale, heading for the financial district with the caravan close behind. When they drove under Freeway 101 and turned down Flower Street, they got their first glimpse of the Dragon Head Building straight ahead on Fifth. Bart felt his stomach squeeze into a knot. It was one thing to view the building from the safe distance of Griffith Park, and quite another to see it up close. The thing towered over all the other buildings. Its windows were dark and menacing. At Third Street, Bart pulled the truck over and the rest of the trucks pulled in behind him. Rollie and Jain jumped off the back of the truck. Their skin now had that lime green glow, and sparks flickered off their hair.

"You guys doin' ok?" Bart asked. "Your eyes are, like, kaleidoscopic. They're almost spinning."

"Never felt better," said Rollie. He took a long stretch and cracked his knuckles.

"I'm good," Jain said. "Why are we stopping?" Are we there?"

Bart pointed ahead. "Look at that street. It's on fire. The trucks will explode if we try to drive on it." Flames leaped out of cracks in the street, and pedestrians ran in panic, hugging the sides of buildings, trying to balance on narrow slices of intact pavement. Some tripped, their skin and clothing singed. Others fell into the flames, screaming. They didn't get up. Bart looked at the men with him, reading their eyes for a reaction. "We'll detour north a few blocks until we find a safe cross street and then take that to Fifth. Then, we'll have to park and proceed on foot. I'll load the seed gun with crystal, and everyone else will carry a bag to resupply me. I will spray the building with crystal. Understood?"

No one looked happy about it, but everyone nodded.

Chapter 8

The Commander of the Mayor's Guard was tall enough that his vest fit TJ perfectly. Gem gave the order to the rest of the soldiers to remove their vests, and they did so without protest. Dean found a vest that could fit around his broad back and shoulders. He helped Willet and Audrey into vests that fit them reasonably well with the side straps tightened. They each took a pair of goggles. Gem took a vest herself, just in case. She blew a Freezing Breath over the soldiers, and they dropped to the ground. The Circle relieved every soldier of helmets and vests and stripped them of their black uniforms. They gave the clothes to Marva to store in the coffee shop in case she or her patrons might need protection. Who knew how many of the mind-altering guns were circulating in the city?

"We cannot leave these guns behind," Gem said. "They are too dangerous in the wrong hands and must be destroyed."

The Circle gathered the guns and put them in a pile. Gem gave a nod to Dora. The big dog opened her mouth and blasted the pile with white-hot flame, reducing the guns to a twisted mess of molten metal.

Sonrisa Degas stepped out of a fold in spacetime like a lightbulb flash and stood in the middle of the street, tall and imposing. She was in military attire, a camouflage shirt, pants, and black boots. As a being who traveled through space and time, her clothing varied with her destination. One never knew how she would look when she arrived. Dark chestnut hair flowed back from her face in soft waves. Her brown eyes were luminous, and her skin glowed as if she had just visited a star. The power in her visage was startling enough to make them stare. Sonrisa raised an eyebrow at the Circle in their vests. "What is this, Guardian? The Circle needs protective garments now?"

"We were under fire," Gem said. "These vests will help us avoid the worst effects if we get hit again."

Sonrisa frowned but then nodded. "I see. Is the boy with you? I hoped he would be here."

"You mean, Jonah?" TJ exclaimed. "He's supposed to be with you!"

"He slipped away and took a ride out of the park with friends of yours," Sonrisa replied. "I believe he was looking for you."

"What friends? We don't have any friends here!" TJ ran anxious fingers through his sandy hair, and his voice rose. "Don't tell me he's in the city!"

"I can only say that he is no longer in the care of his mother and Arhat."

TJ started to pace. Willet tried to calm him, but there wasn't much encouragement she could give under the circumstances. "Maybe he didn't come this way."

"Oh, he's coming here, alright. After I told him to stay put. He's all about 'helping' me do Circle stuff!"

"What friends are you talking about, Sonrisa?" Gem asked. "Did they give names?"

"One called himself Bart. He said he knew Dean and Audrey, and there were two men with him. Arhat told him you were headed into the city."

"If Jonah is with Bart, he should be ok," Dean said. "Bart's a decent guy, he'll look after Jonah. The only reason Bart would go to Griffith Park is to find us, and I bet he has crystal with him."

"He had a truck with many bags in the hold," replied Sonrisa. "A strong energy came from them."

"Excellent," Dean said. "Just what we need."

Veins stood out on TJ's neck as he fumed. "So, they *are* coming this way. We have to find them before they get too close to that building. Matt Gregg will use Jonah as a bargaining tool if he gets his claws into him. Not to mention, we need to find some damn dynamite!"

"Sonrisa," Gem said, "if you please, we must go to the Dragon Head. No time to waste."

The Traveler opened a fold in spacetime, and Gem and the Circle stepped in. If anyone was watching at that moment, they would see six people disappear into thin air, a coffee shop with a blown-out front door, a pile of smoking melted metal, and twelve men lying in the street in their underwear.

*****

Bart and the caravan found a cross street that was free of fire and took it to Fifth Street. The caravan stopped. Everyone got out of the trucks and took a good look at the Dragon Head Building that loomed straight ahead. The black stone building stared back at them. Its blank windows were like sightless eyes. The men grumbled. 'That place looks haunted." "How close do we have to get to it?" "Not sure I should be here. I have a family."

"The US Bank Building used to sit on that very spot," Rollie said, waving his green hands at it. "I did pharmacy business there. How could this monstrosity be in its place like the old bank never existed?"

Bart had no explanations and didn't try to make one up. Besides, they had other problems. On the long street in front of them, ten helmeted members of the Mayor's Guard were herding a line of people with ropes around their necks toward the Dragon Head Building. It was the experience Nick and Jain had described to him. In that moment, he had a keen sense that he had led other people into a suicide mission. If they got hurt or worse, it was on his head, but it was too late to change his mind. He needed their help. Shouldering the seed gun filled with crystal chips, he had Rollie at one shoulder and Jain at the other. They stalked silently down the street toward the prisoners and stopped at a safe distance.

"What are we gonna do?" Bart murmured. "We have to get past them."

Jain's fingers were green and glowing from the crystal. They curled into fists. "Let me at those guards," he snarled. "I'll make 'em wish they never touched me."

"I'm with you," Rollie whispered. "Stay low and quiet, be quick. Aim for the legs."

Two guards led at the front of the line, and two brought up the rear. Three guards marched single file to the left of the line and three more to the right. The element of surprise was in their favor, so Rollie and Jain crouched down and crept up behind the line. They slid their glowing hands up the pants legs of the back guards. When their hands touched skin, the guards' bodies convulsed as if they were electrocuted. Rollie and Jain caught them and laid them quietly on the ground. Prisoners at the back of the line turned to look. Rollie motioned to them to stay quiet while Jain moved on to the guards marching on the right. He rolled in on the ground and grabbed the legs of two guards at the same time, finding skin. They both dropped heavily, leaving the third guard looking around for the reason. Jain wrapped an arm around his ankles and slid a hand up his pant leg. The guard shuddered and fell. Rollie headed for the guards on the left and crouched. As soon as he touched them, they dropped like dead weight. The third guard whirled on Rollie, raising his gun. Rollie lowered his shoulder and knocked the guard over, finishing him off with a green zap to the neck.

After that, the element of surprise was lost, but they had the remaining guards wrong-footed. All the prisoners were alert now, shouting and ducking their heads, expecting gun fire. Rollie and Jain dropped and rolled toward the front, using the confusion of the prisoners as cover. The guards were looking at the prisoners and didn't see them coming until it was too late. When they were close enough, Rollie and Jain grabbed the guards by the legs and yanked them off their feet. Shocks to the legs had them jerking and quivering until they went still. The prisoners disentangled themselves from the neck ropes, and with quick nods of thanks, ran off into the darkness of the streets. There was the question of the guns lying on the ground next to the fallen guards. What to do with them?

"They don't shoot regular bullets," Rollie said. "Maybe just for visual effect, like mine."

"I don't care what they shoot," Jain said. He picked up a gun and looked down the trumpet-shaped barrel. "This is a weird looking gun."

"Lower that thing! It could release poison gas, or an explosive, or something," Rollie said. "We don't want to make a lot of noise and have the rest of the Guard down on our heads. We should put the damn things where they can't be found. There's a dumpster over there. Let's dump 'em."

"Not so fast." Jain quickly reversed the gun in his hands, aimed at a fallen guard and fired. Whatever came out of the gun hit the vest-covered chest of the guard. He didn't so much as twitch.

Jain looked disappointed. "Military-type guys wouldn't carry these guns if they didn't do something. I'm guessing the vest protected him. We should take vests and helmets for ourselves. Just to be safe."

Jain took the fallen guard's helmet and put it on his own head, then pulled the vest off and strapped it around his chest. Bart and Rollie removed vests from two other guards. It couldn't hurt to wear them. Jain picked up the gun again and shot the same guard in the chest. This time he jerked when the gunfire hit him. There was no bullet.

Jain raised a fist in victory. "See? I knew it."

"Are you satisfied now?" Rollie said, glaring at him.

Jain glared back. "I'd be satisfied if I knew they were all dead."

He knelt and poked a finger into the ribs of the guard he shot. The guy's eyes opened and gave Jain a blank stare. "The gun didn't kill him. It's a stun gun like they used on Nick and me. We should keep 'em."

"No guns," Rollie said. "Guns are unpredictable."

"Nobody made *you* the boss, Zeemer, not that I'm aware."

Edgar Zeemer, Chuck Tomasek and Clarence Duggins came over from the caravan and helped themselves to helmets and vests while Rollie and Bart gathered up nine guns and shoved them in among the bags of trash in the dumpster. Jain kept the tenth gun despite objections from Rollie.

Bart breathed a sigh of relief. It could have been worse. "Ok, guys, we've made our presence known. Let's go find Dean and Company." With seed gun and bags of crystal in hand, they marched down Fifth Street like they were soldiers themselves. Bart hoped no one would question them before they reached the Dragon Head Building.

Chapter 9

The implacable Queen of Deserts draws sunlight to her breast, exhales long, slow breaths of restless wind into drifting clouds, and whispers, "surrender". Her heat stifles resistance. Heads bow and knees bend. In the swish of sand blowing across hard ground, the dry scourge scrubs away all that should not be and leaves the land bare. The King of Seas roars and rolls, spreads towering waves and bites deep into the dry, empty land, devouring his fill. With his hunger satisfied, he spumes white froth into mist. The tang of salt hangs in the air. A new world is born under the sea.

"Where are we going?" Willet said. With the Traveler moving them, they could be going literally anywhere.

"We are going to the Dragon Head Building," Gem said. "The sooner we confront Jat and stop his assault, the better."

Sonrisa Degas traveled by folding spacetime, touching one point in space and time to another to form a short corridor. She had explained that long ago to the Circle. Travel was a matter of walking into one end of the corridor and out the other. How she managed this was impossible to figure out from watching her. She stood with eyes closed, hummed HU, and spoke other words in Spanish. The air hummed with her, and then a door in spacetime folded open, leading into a different place. Or sometimes, time sped by, and they ended up in the same place but at a different time. In any case, the trip was usually instantaneous and dizzying. This didn't feel like other trips they had taken with the Traveler. The movement was more jolt than flow. Momentum swung forward and back and forward again until everyone felt queasy. Suddenly, they were suspended in midair, their feet dangling.

"A bit of flux and uncertainty," Sonrisa said. "A void could be forming here."

"The floating is nice," Willet said. "It's quiet too. The voices are gone."

"That will not last, unfortunately," Sonrisa told her.

Movement resumed in a hard lurch and dropped everyone unceremoniously on their behinds except the Traveler who landed lightly on her feet. Voices once again clamored and cried and whispered like the Tower of Babel, hitting Willet's ears in a barrage. She used her developing skill of controlling the vibration of her ear drums to bring the cacophony down to a bearable level. She tried to tune in to individual voices and conversations, hoping for a clue as to what is happening at that time, but there was too much noise to understand much. Then there were periods of absolute silence, which Willet reported to the Traveler. Voices, or lack of them, gave an indication of what was out there and when it might not be safe to step off the TimeTrack.,

"We have encountered an anomaly in spacetime," Sonrisa announced. "The future of the city is not final, so we experience what you might think of as temporal turbulence. It can be unsettling."

"Unsettling indeed," Gem said, picking herself up. "Can we move beyond this?"

"My apologies, Guardian. When the Walls converged on Los Angeles, the city stood still in time. If the city falls into the Underworld, it will cease to move forward in present time and will detour onto a different time path. On the other hand, if the Circle prevents the fall, the city will rejoin its normal flow of time and continue on the expected path. The future path is undecided. Thus, we are in a State of Flux around this point."

"That sort of makes sense," Dean said. "The future is open. It's not predetermined, but I don't get how spacetime could ever be interrupted. How is that even possible?"

"When something exists in time and then ceases to exist altogether, it reaches the edge of a cliff in time and, in a sense, falls off. The main flow of time leaves that dead end behind and continues on without it."

"Has this happened before?" Gem asked.

Sonrisa nodded. "Many worlds and civilizations have come and gone, leaving no trace."

"But we were just there, standing in the street," TJ said. "L.A. still existed. We could go back to that time, couldn't we? And stop the fall, however that will work."

"This makes *no* sense," Audrey said, rubbing her temples. "There have been civilizations on earth for hundreds of thousands of years. We still know about them even though they're gone."

"A civilization is not only pot shards and arrowheads or crumbled buildings," the Traveler said. "The essence of a people is their State of Consciousness, their language, ideas, and images. Many more civilizations have existed than we know. Their essence has been lost to us. Their future was not our future."

"Doesn't that break a basic law of physics?" Dean said. "Energy can't be created or destroyed."

"If a civilization diverges from the present flow of time, it continues on a new path, not destroyed, but unreachable from our own path. They are in parallel."

"Maybe it's like a black hole in space," Dean said. "Stars get sucked in and disappear. The gravity of the black hole is so intense that not even light can escape. Maybe some part of what goes in there joins a different time track, except for the Hawking radiation, of course. That energy escapes." He was warming up to one of his favorite subjects in physics. "Or is this the quantum multiverse? Multiple universes existing simultaneously at every point in time. Maybe a time track can leave one universe and join a another."

TJ's eyes were rolling. "Man, stop it. You are such a geek."

Sonrisa nodded at Dean. "You grasp the concept, even if the exact explanation is not yet known to this world. We must find the point in time before the city left this time track and locate the building before it disappears. Then we can intervene. If not…" She shrugged.

"What do we do about it?" TJ asked. "Have we failed? Is everyone doomed?"

"We will try everything," Gem said. "Until there is nothing left to try."

"What happens if we get off at the wrong stop?" Willet said. "Can *we* get disconnected from present time?"

"A reasonable question," Sonrisa said. "Unfortunately, the answer is yes."

Travel on the Time Track inched forward, irritatingly slow. When Sonrisa finally opened the next fold in spacetime, a strange, frightening sight confronted them. The Dragon Head Building was absorbing people, buildings, streets, cars and trees, all like so much water. Whatever it absorbed left streaks of color in the stone.

"It's like a giant sponge," Audrey said. "I can't believe what I'm seeing."

"The building drinks in the essence of the city, leaving nothing behind," Gem said.

The rising edge of colors crept up the walls of the Dragon Head Building as it soaked up the city. People ran in panic, unsure which way to go before the absorbing force of the building took them. There seemed to be no way to avoid it. Their terror and demise was horrifying to watch.

The Time Track sped up again and then stopped. A fold in spacetime opened onto the same scene, but now the city looked as if it were scrubbed clean. The few people and buildings that remained were bleached white. People stood frozen as in a tableau. At the next stop in time, the Dragon Head Building had broken free of the ground and was spinning in place like an enormous top, picking up speed and throwing off shafts of black glittering reflection. A chasm opened underneath the foundation, and the massive structure dropped into it until the top of the building disappeared beneath the ground, taking whatever was left of Los Angeles with it. The physical existence of the city was gone, erased, nothing there except a dull empty space.

"This is the way it will end," Gem murmured. "This is Jat's plan, not to destroy the city in a pit of fire, but to erase it from the physical plane, leaving nothing behind."

Watching it happen left the Circle shocked and heavy-hearted. "What will happen to the people?" Willet said. "They don't deserve this, not most of them. They still have light."

"Most souls will move on to the astral to wait until they begin another incarnation," Gem said. "Some will rise to higher worlds. Others will find themselves in the Underworld nightmare that Jat has prepared for them."

"But now we know how and when the city comes to an end on the time track," Dean said. "That's good, right? Like TJ said. We just have to reverse course and go back to the beginning when all this started and then stop the whole thing from starting."

Sonrisa closed the fold in spacetime, and the time track edged backward, but then suddenly lurched forward and backward in crazy fits and starts as if it was slipping on ice. Everyone clung to each other, trying to stay on their feet. When the movement stopped, the Traveler could not open a doorway.

"We are in a void," she said. "We cannot maneuver here. Between the end of one world and the beginning of another, there is no space or time. Where we would go from here is uncertain and dangerous"

"I must confer with the Elements of Mother Earth," Gem said. "Ocean and Desert will take possession of the void and fill it with water and sand. I must convince them to wait long enough for us to stop the city's disappearance. Take me to them, Traveler."

The track raced forward again to the edge of the void and then stopped just as abruptly. This time, Sonrisa was able to open a doorway. They looked out into a driving rainstorm over an ocean. Waves of dark water roiled and crashed. Storm clouds rolled in the sky, with rumbling thunder and spikes of lightning. Gem and Sonrisa looked at each other and communicated their unspoken thoughts.

"I have to try," Gem replied to the question in the Traveler's eyes.

"Guardian, no, it is too dangerous," Sonrisa said. "You know how the Ocean King is. He is deaf to reason."

"Yes, but if there is a chance of stopping him, I must take it."

The Traveler reluctantly opened a doorway. Gem stood at the open door and filled her lungs with wet ocean air. When she exhaled, her breath hit the surface of the choppy water and hardened into a platform of floating ice. Without a word, she stepped into the storm and walked across the ice she had created. A mewl of worry came out of Dora. The Circle murmured. "What is she doing?" "This is nuts." Even their experience with the amazing ways of the Guardian couldn't ease their concern for her.

Gem stopped on the ice several yards out and waved her arms above her head. The chunk of ice she stood on bucked so hard they thought she might slide into the water, but she kept her balance and road it like a surfboard. A giant wave of water rose in front of her, reached a towering height enough to swamp her, and hovered over her, suspended. It looked like the wave might swallow her at any moment. Sea foam crested over its apex and splattered down into the water. Gem shouted at the wave. They couldn't hear anything she said for all crashing of waves, but the giant wall of water remained, hanging over her. After several minutes of manic conversation, the wave curled backward and dropped into the ocean with a great splash. Gem made her way across the ice and back to the doorway as sedately as she left.

"Well," asked Sonrisa. "What did he say?"

"The King of Oceans is lost to the ecstasy of his flood. I think he heard me. He did not reply, but the waves are dying down. I hope this means he has decided to give us a little time."

The fold in spacetime sealed shut, and the passage of time picked up speed like a runaway train. When it stopped, a fold opened on flat, empty land in the grip of a sandstorm. To step into it would be treacherous. Sonrisa's attire changed into a sapphire blue cloak that reached to her toes. She pulled the hood of her cloak over her head and stepped into the hot winds. Gem swirled a globe of transparent ice around herself, Dora, and the Circle to protect them from flying sand, and they all stepped through the doorway together. It was so hot that the surface of the globe began to sweat immediately. The source of the storm proved to be a swirling cylinder of sand seven feet tall throwing off spirals of sand into undulating piles. The wind blew the sand out across the bare land. Dunes were forming in all directions, the beginnings of a great desert.

"Queen of the Desert," Gem called out, "please stay your hand. We will save this place from the void."

The cylinder was actually a woman wearing a white sheath dress. Her copper skin and lavender quartz eyes glowed against the shimmering satin of the dress, and her long dark brown hair blew wild in the wind. She stood on the toes of her bare feet and twirled, controlling the whip of the winds with waves of her hands and arms. Sand flew from her fingers. When the woman heard Gem's voice, she stopped her twirl, and the sandstorm died down. Her face was handsome but severe, with high sculpted cheekbones.

She spoke through dry lips in a voice like the hiss of sand rushing over stone. "The void must be filled, Guardian. I take what is mine as the King of Oceans makes his claim under water. Fire will consume, and wind will have its way. This space cannot remain unmade. Form must manifest."

Gem let her globe of ice melt away. "We respect your right, oh Queen. The King of Oceans has paused his flood. If we cannot redirect the past, then you will have your share."

The Desert Queen gave a dry chuckle. "King Ocean does not always keep his word when his waves are high. You know this."

"Give us a little time. That is all we ask."

The Queen pursed her lips and gave them an undecipherable stare. Lights gleamed from her eyes sharp enough to cut diamonds. "Very well, Guardian," she said. "I will wait, but I will not wait long. The void calls to me like a siren. I must fill it. The land was nearly mine before the void took it, when the water disappeared. It should be mine by right." She folded her arms over her head and turned into a column of sand that scattered in the wind and disappeared.

"The Queen is impatient," Gem said. "There is little time to prevent her from re-creating the desert. We must find our way back to the beginning, as our Warrior suggested, before the building began its spin."

"You saw the unpredictability of the time track, Guardian," Sonrisa replied. "Finding our way back to a precise moment in time so close to a void could be perilous. The risk to the Circle is great."

"Wait, what now?" Audrey and Willet looked at each other. "What risk?"

"We do not know how long it took for the city to be erased completely. It might have happened in an instant, over many days, years, or centuries."

"Why does that matter?" TJ asked.

"The speed and length of regression to the past from this point in time might be too great for you to survive. Or we might enter a temporal dead end from which we cannot escape. Either eventuality could be hazardous to the continued existence of your current physical incarnation."

No one liked the sound of that. "Can we get a do-over?" Audrey mumbled.

"What can we do to return to the right place?" Gem said, her voice tinged with impatience. "That is the main question."

"We could go back to a time before the building even appeared on the street, so we can prevent the whole situation," Dean said. "Is that possible?"

"Jat is not constrained by space or time," Gem said. "His building is an apparition. He can place it on any street at any time. If we change the past and protect the whole of Fifth Avenue, then he will simply create his building on another street. We must see the building in place to be sure we can destroy it."

Sonrisa nodded. "I will attempt to bring us to a time before the city fell but after the Dragon Head Building appeared on the street. Finding it will be as difficult as shooting an arrow into the sea to catch a fish. I make no guarantee."

"That doesn't sound promising," TJ said. "Isn't there a way to increase the odds in our favor?"

The Traveler gave him a solemn look. "The universe is over thirteen billion years old, Warrior. One moment looks much like another."

"So we travel back in time and hope we reach the right spot," Gem said, looking into the eyes of each member of her Circle. "There is no other alternative."

They all nodded at her. It was the only choice they had. The time track reversed and rolled backward through ages of empty darkness, sometimes shifted forward at light speed, and then backwards again. The forces of shifting momentum had them gasping for breath. It seemed like the trip would never end, but finally the ride slowed. Adjustments had to be made delicately. Sonrisa opened fold after fold, inching backward and forward in time. They saw the Dragon Head Building spinning through one doorway. It was shaking in the next doorway, and it wasn't there at all in the doorway after that. Sonrisa put a break on the track and moved it backward until she zeroed in on a moment when the building was in place and intact on Fifth Avenue, but before it began to spin. The time track jolted to a stop. Sonrisa quickly opened a fold before the opportunity was lost.

They stepped out of the doorway on wobbling legs onto cracked streets and smoking concrete. Tongues of fire lapped up between the cracks. Large square buildings and towering skyscrapers on both sides of the streets were covered with soot. The heavy, acrid smell of Sulphur hung in the air. Through the blinding flashes of static, they stepped over broken sidewalks to avoid the flames licking at their feet through the cracks.

Across the street, two hooded figures engaged in a knife fight. They stalked and stabbed at each other. Knife metal clinked and glinted in the fiery gloom. One fighter's arm hung uselessly at his side. The other limped.

A passerby walking on that side of the street saw the fight and stumbled off the curb trying to avoid it. The fighters turned on him with knives held high, ready to pounce. Another passerby jumped into the street and dragged the man away to the other side of the street where they both regained balance and hurried away in the opposite direction. Good thing. The Circle was not prepared to intervene in a knife fight.

The last time they saw the Dragon Head Building, it was light grey stone like many of the downtown buildings around it. Now the huge walls seemed to ripple like living snakeskin, black and shiny, and looked about to spring out of the ground. Gem, Sonrisa and the Circle walked toward the building in tight formation. The air, stale and burnt, was full of pollution and barely breathable. Audrey threw up a light ring and expanded it to drop protectively around them. They reached the front of the Dragon Head Building and looked in through the glass doors. The lobby was dark and empty.

"We still need dynamite," TJ said backing away from the door. "I should go look for some."

Gem spoke quietly to her Circle. "We need to enter the building to see who and what is in there. If there are innocents inside, they must be moved to a safe place before we attempt any destruction."

"I'm not going in there," TJ said. "Just can't do it."

"But you're the one who knows the building best," Dean said.

"I know the building too," Willet said. "I've been inside."

"Not physically, you haven't," TJ snarled. "You can't go in there, Willet. No way. I won't allow it."

"This mission will require sacrifices," Gem continued. "Our Steel Warrior should enter the building from the ground floor, much as it distresses him. He *is* the most familiar with it. The Listener will go with him, but only in her Light body. She will provide information to him through her finer senses. Ring Thrower and Golden Heart will secure access to the roof. If there is opposition, create a diversion until the building can be cleared. The Traveler will assist you. Are these directions clear?"

"Where will you be, Gem?" Audrey asked.

"I must confer with Augustus, and then I will quickly return. When the battle starts, I will be at your side, have no doubt."

Gem disappeared in her usual abrupt way and took Dora with her this time. Sonrisa whisked Dean and Audrey into a fold in spacetime and they disappeared too, leaving TJ and Willet standing in front of the glass doors of the Dragon Head Building. They looked again into the dark lobby, and then at each other. No dynamite. Now what?

"Dean and Audrey will be on the roof," TJ said. "I'll get in and meet them somewhere on the inside. With intel from you, we'll locate any people and get them out. Quick and easy."

"You can do it, babe," Willet said and kissed his cheek. "I'll be with you."

*****

Augustus stood in front of the Map of World Consciousness and studied the activity displayed there when Gem and Dora appeared in his office. Los Angeles County was in a State of Upheaval. Gray clouds turned black on the map and spread beyond downtown. Parts of the city throbbed blood red with extreme emotions.

"We saw the future," Gem said. "Los Angeles disappears. Are we too late to change it?"

"My dear, there are many paths into the future," Augustus said. "Until a path is taken, there is time to choose another. Jat will attack your Circle's every weakness. He will foster anger, fear, despair. Even lust. If that fails, he will threaten. All his ploys must be ignored. Can they do this?"

"The Circle knows what is at stake. They protect each other. I trust them."

"He will try to divert their attention from the main objective."

"How?"

"The fight against the Deceiver is a puzzle. The pieces are scattered. The Circle must recognize the pieces when they see them and assemble them into the correct picture."

"This is not a game, Augustus. My people are inside that building. If it collapses, they will perish. I need more guidance."

Augustus placed his hands on Gem's shoulders and looked into her eyes. "The Circle has reached Jat's fortress despite formidable obstacles of time and unknowing. This is a victory. The forces of Light and Sound are already with them, and the Deceiver has sown the seeds of his own destruction. Do not lose heart. Inspire your Circle and lead them as you do so well. With your help, they will prevail."

Chapter 10

Dean and Audrey stepped out of a fold in spacetime onto the flat, open space at the top of the Dragon Head Building. The granite chair, Jat's throne, was still there. A much smaller man sat in it. He had a reptile's claw for a left hand and two webbed reptilian feet. The pupils of his yellow eyes were slitted, and a snake's tongue flickered between his lips.

He hissed when the Circle members suddenly appeared in front of his chair. "How dare you come before me unannounced?" the man said. "I am Mayor of Los Angeles. What is your business?"

"Matt Gregg, is that you?" Dean asked, looking him over in astonishment. "You've really changed."

"I evolved," replied Matt the Mayor, giving them a slow reptilian blink. "The Great One empowered me. Who are you?"

"It's me, Dean, TJ's friend. Audrey too. We met, remember?"

"Ah yes. I remember," Matt hissed again. "Your friendship with Barlow wins you no favor with me."

"Why are you sitting up here?" Audrey said.

"It is my right," he sniffed. "I have no time for your silly questions, little girl. Do not provoke my anger."

Audrey laughed. "I'm not a little girl, lizard man. You shouldn't provoke my anger either."

Dean gave her a side glance with arched eyebrow. "Have you lost your mind?" he murmured. "Remember what we're here for."

"I'm tired of Jat's puppets trying to intimidate me, Dean" she said. "Really tired of it."

Matt Gregg watched this exchange with a smirk of amusement. "What *are* you here for, hmmm? I'm ready for a good laugh."

"We're going to bring this building down," Dean said. "Destroy it. You don't want to be up here when that happens."

Matt glared at them. "Are you threatening me? I'll cut you both to ribbons where you stand."

Audrey gave him a sour smile. "I have big-girl weapons. You won't be laughing when I'm done with you."

The slitted reptilian eyes narrowed. "This conversation has made me hungry," he snapped his fingers and called out, "Georgina, a bite, please, and there's something here for you to enjoy also."

Seconds later, a long black appendage curled up behind the granite chair and stepped delicately onto the roof, followed by another leg, followed by the body of a spider as big as a horse. It crept up beside Matt and regurgitated something yellow and foul from its mouth into a disgusting splat beside the throne.

"Ah, thank you, my dear," said Matt Gregg. "I believe you know these two. Take your pick."

The mottled brown and black coloring on the spider body and black-bristled hair on its legs were uncomfortably familiar. Lady G. in her spider form. The spider launched herself at them. Dean stepped in front of Audrey and spread his arms wide to protect her, but the spider moved in fast. She wrapped her long front legs around his shoulders, yanked him toward herself and stuffed him into her mouth head first. Just as quickly, the arachnid scuttled backward and dropped off the back of the building.

"Dean!" Audrey shouted. She ran to the edge of the roof and looked down.

The spider was hanging upside down by a long thread attached to the roof, casually stretching her legs in the air with Dean clamped in her mouth. It was a *long* way down to the ground. If Audrey threw a ring at her, the spider might drop him.

Audrey whirled to face the reptile. "Bring him back! Make her bring him back right now or you'll be sorry!"

"More threats?" Matt chuckled. "You're a lousy negotiator. There's something I want in return for my good will. Bring TJ Barlow to me. We have a score to settle. I owe him for the loss of my hand. When he's under my control, you can have your man back but do it soon. Lady G likes to eat her meat fresh."

Audrey stalked back to the granite chair and stared at the lizard man with heat in her eyes. She was done with diplomacy. "TJ won't be joining us, you freak," she said in a low snarl. A small ring formed in her right palm. The ring heated her flesh all the way up her arm. She let it get hot, hotter, until her skin began to cook. There would be scars on her palm, but she didn't care. She backed up a few steps to give herself room for a throw.

When Matt saw the ring, he spread his palms in front of him. Several razor blades floated between his hands, edges shining. He smiled. "Want to play catch? I'm very good at it. Maybe you'll like to catch these."

The razor blades flew at her so fast she didn't have time to do more than throw her right arm up and hide her face in her elbow. The sharp edges sliced across her arm. She felt the sting of multiple cuts and blood began to flow. Two cuts on her forehead oozed and dripped down to her eyes. Fury burned even hotter as she wiped blood out of her eyes. The razor blades flew back to Matt's hands. He held them a moment, suspended between his palms, and they flew again like a swarm of wasps. She ducked low this time. The blades skimmed over her hair, then flew back to Matt. He readied another throw.

She turned the ring on its edge. It expanded and hovered in front of her like a shield of light. The next flurry of blades hit the shield and ricocheted off, falling harmlessly to the roof with a clink. Matt turned his magnetic palms out and gathered the blades back. In the moments he readied his little slicers for another attack, Audrey flipped her shield flat, grabbed the edge in a frisbee hold and hurled it at him with a strong flick of the wrist.

The sharp, hot edge of the shield hit Matt in the neck and sliced through it like a meat cleaver through salami. His head rolled off his shoulders, and his body slumped backward into the chair. The head bounced onto the roof, tongue still flicking between his lips, slitted yellow eyes blinking in surprise. The tongue soon stopped flicking. Blood fountained from the neck of his torso and drenched his shirt.

Audrey watched the light dim in those yellow eyes. "I have a stronger throw than you, and a better defense," she said. "Didn't see that coming, did ya." The elation of the fight swelled within her and then drained away. Her skin chilled with the shock.

"I killed Matt Gregg."

The enormity of it froze her.

She flashed back to the first time she saw Matt standing in TJ's office in a shirt and tie, shuffling papers like the businessman he once was. "TJ's friend. He was just a normal guy when I met him." She shivered at the consequences of her actions, killing on reflex, without thinking twice. *I'm guilty of murder.* Her arm ached, and the cuts burned. Blood and cuts were the least of her concerns, but she had to wrap the arm somehow to keep the cuts from re-opening. All she had was the sleeve of her shirt rolled up to her elbow. She pulled it down to the wrist and pressed the fabric into the bloody wounds, so sore she wanted to scream. It would be difficult to throw rings with that arm.

Jat twisted Matt Gregg into something less than human. He would twist her too if she wasn't careful. Her head felt too big on her neck. Lights from somewhere stabbed into her eyes. She raised her hand to block the glare. Her head ached, and then everything blurred around her. When the lights cleared, she was standing in an empty room in front of seven figures lined up on a raised platform. A black hooded robe draped each figure, men seven feet tall and made of gray stone, hands tucked into wide sleeves. An icy laser light beamed from each pair of eyes, all directed at her.

The Stone Lords again?

These were the same big statues she saw lining the long corridor in her dream. "What do you want?" she asked out loud. "And stop staring at me."

A high voice chimed through the room. "You must have representation to address the Stone Lords. This is a court of law," he said.

A pale, thin man in a white suit with a shock of white hair stepped out from behind the statues. Thick white circles of light spun around his eyes, and small ice blue bulbs glowed from his eye sockets, directing beams of silver-blue light right at her.

She felt the beams dart over her face. They left tracings on her skin that stung cold. Audrey couldn't stop staring into those spinning white circles. *Is this the weirdest thing I've seen today? Maybe not, it's been a long day.* There were more pressing matters to deal with. "Why am I in a court?" she asked.

"You have taken a life," said the man. "I present the case, and The Stone Lords judge."

Her irritation rose. "They have no right to judge me. That person was trying to hurt me. He cut up my arm. I acted in self-defense."

"Do you not feel the guilt?" the ghostly lawyer said softly. "Does the weight of it crush you?"

"I don't feel great about it, but I had no choice."

Voices rumbled out of the stone figures. "Present the evidence," one voice said. "She took a life," replied a deeper voice. "A punishable offense." "She has admitted her own guilt," said a third.

"The judgement is made," the first voice said. "Her soul is forfeit."

What? "I object!" she said. "When do I get my rebuttal?"

Gripped by anxiety, she struggled to breathe, looking at her own wide-eyed reflection in a huge mirror. The stone statues loomed in the mirror, too, behind her reflection. She looked behind her, but the statues weren't there. *Am I here or there?* Either she was in two places at once or split between two worlds. She touched her thumb to the surface of the mirror. It melted into rain drops. Lightning flashed painfully through her skull, and a voice laughed. "Humans are puppets."

She was overcome by a splitting headache, but Audrey refused to become a puppet. "You can't take my soul!" she shouted. "No one can. You're a liar!"

In an instant, she was back on the roof in front of the granite chair. The body of the lizard man still sat slumped in the chair with his head laying at his feet, as she had left it.
Omygod. I really did this.

She struggled to remember why she was there. *Dean!* She ran to the edge of the roof and looked down. The height made her head swim. She had to pull back and take a deep breath to steady herself, then peeked over the edge again. The spider was still hanging off the side of the building with Dean struggling in her mouth. All Audrey could see were his legs flailing as he tried to free himself. A hopeful sign – he was still alive and fighting – but she wanted him to calm down before he slipped out of the spider's mouth. If he fell, would the Traveler be able to catch him? He might die of a heart attack before he hit the ground. She didn't want to test the spider's reflexes. *Don't drop him, don't drop him.* She hoped Georgina couldn't hear her thoughts. She might drop him just for spite.

Revulsion turned her stomach, and anger burned like acid in her veins. "I won't hesitate to kill you next time, bitch," she spit through her teeth. The spider scrambled into a large window below the roof and disappeared with Dean still firmly in her maw.

"Your point is made, Ring Thrower," the Traveler's voice came from behind her. "Your assistance is needed inside."

"Take me there," she said and hurried to the Traveler's side, "before she tries to eat him. She went in through a window below the roof. They'll be on the top floor."

*****

Bart, Jain, and Rollie reached the Dragon Head Building, but no one from the Circle was there. The men stood in front of the huge monolith and stared at it uncertainly, then at the seed gun in Bart's hands, then back at the building. "OK," Rollie said. "What do we do?"

"What I know about this crystal is that it eats pollution," Bart said. "I have no idea if it will do anything to this building. That was supposed to be Dean's call."

"Well, let's shoot a few rounds and see what happens," Rollie said. "We have to get inside to find Robbie."

Bart emptied his seed gun full of crystal at the base of the building. Rollie handed him another bag. He refilled the gun and peppered the walls with chips. Bag after bag of crystal fell at the feet of the building and built up in sparkling piles. Bart held his hand out to Jain for another bag.

Rollie murmured in his ear. "Don't you want to stop a minute and see if the chips are doing anything? We're down to half a truck load."

A reasonable idea. Bart paused and studied the black behemoth. It seemed unperturbed by the crystal laying around its feet. Were they using the crystal in the wrong way? Maybe they should set it on fire first. Rollie and Jain, along with the rest of Rollie's crew, gathered beside Bart to discuss their next move.

Edgar Zeemer gave the building a killing stare. "Why don't we just break through the glass? I'll run in and search for my son. You guys take down any goons that come out. Then we get out fast."

"I'm not sure we'll be able to 'take down the goons' if there are a lot of them, Ed," Rollie told his brother. "We don't have any real weapons, just the one weird gun that Jain took from the guard. I know you want to find Robbie, but we need to think through a real plan."

"That building looks like a firetrap," Chief Duggins said, scratching at his beard. "Multi-story, only one ground floor exit, no fire escapes. If a fire starts in there, it would be almost impossible to get out from the upper floors. We don't have equipment for catching people if they jump."

"It looks dark in there," Bart said. "Hard to tell if anyone's in there."

"*We'll* be in there," Major Tomasek said. "Charging into a building when we don't know what's inside could get us killed. We need intel. I'll go in on reconnaissance with one other person. Who's with me?" Edgar raised his hand. "Good," the Marine said. "Follow me and guard our six."

Tomasek handed Edgar one of the knives he had in his belt. The two men peered through the glass doors. Edgar kicked his steel-toed boot at the door. It had no effect. He kicked harder and then slammed the sole of his boot against the door with the full force of his leg behind it. The door rattled but stood firm. He threw the bulk of his body against the door and then kicked at the wall beside it. The stone crumbled into sand, leaving a small hole. Edgar kept kicking. The hole in the stone grew bigger, twice as big as a man's foot

Bart peered inside the hole. "The crystal is eating through the stone, reducing it to sand. This is something, at least, but we don't have enough crystal to eat the whole building."

"Let the crystal keep eating." Rollie said. "If we make an opening big enough, someone could crawl through to the inside and unlock the door."

Bart kicked a toe at the wall. "It would take a while to make a man-sized hole through a wall as thick as this. Not sure we have that kind of time."

"My son is in there!" Edgar exclaimed. "This is taking too long! Get out of my way!" He kicked at the wall until sweat ran down his face, and his chest heaved. The kicking crumbled several superficial layers of stone, but the hole still wasn't big enough or deep enough for a man to crawl through to the inside of the building.

Rollie put his arm around his brother's shoulders. "Ed, calm down, you'll hurt your knee. If there's a way to get in, we'll find it. You don't have to do it alone."

"I have a shovel in my truck," Bart said. "I'll keep digging at the hole to help it along. Or we could take the doors apart. Anyone bring screwdrivers and wrenches?"

A rumbling sound behind them distracted them from the hole and made them spin around. A dark cloud hovered over the street, only yards away. It smelled of burnt flesh. The cloud swirled suddenly and then took the shape of a man in a black undertaker's suit and top hat, with the clawed feet of a lizard below the cuffs of his pants. He was ten feet tall and had the chalk-colored complexion of a bloodless corpse except for the burning coals of malice in his eyes. Under his left arm, he held Jonah squirming in an iron grip. His right arm wrapped around Nick's neck. Nick's mouth was open and gasping for breath.

The man tightened his hold on the struggling bodies. "Be still," he said in a low growl. Jonah and Nick went limp.

Jain raised his trumpet-shaped gun and aimed at the man. "Hey, let them go, mofo, or I'll shoot you!" he shouted. "Who are you?"

The man's thick black lips turned into a leer, and block-shaped teeth emerged from the mirthless grin. His voice boomed down the street. "I am Jat, Lord of the Underworld. This building is mine. You have damaged it. I will take these souls as recompense."

Jat lifted Nick and Jonah above his head as if they were weightless. His body turned back into dark mist and filled the street. A sudden wind blew the mist at the glass doors of the Dragon Head, passed right through, and disappeared inside, leaving the men looking at an empty street.

It happened so quickly that Jain never had a chance to fire his gun. He ran to the doors and banged on the glass with his fists in rage. "Give him back! Nick!"

The doors did not yield. Jain pounded until his fists bruised. He threw his shoulder at the door over and over until he sunk to the ground in a groaning heap.

"JJ, this will get us nowhere," Bart said. "We have to get in another way. Let's get more crystal and keep digging. We need more shovels and tools."

*****

In a parallel time, TJ was yanking on the chrome handles of the Dragon Head Building's glass doors. They were locked. He kicked at the glass, then kicked harder. It was like kicking a rock. He backed up and ran at it, jumped up and kicked the door with both feet. Not a crack.

"I'm going in with you," Willet said, hugging her arms around her chest. "No matter what Gem says. I don't want to be out here by myself."

"I'm not sure either one of us is going in there. This is mutant glass. It doesn't break."

"If Gem were here, she could hurl an ice brick at it."

TJ leaned against the wall next to the door and lifted his foot. "I feel this ankle swelling. Maybe we could climb in a window..."

"You're hurt," she said. "Let me look."

"It's nothing, don't worry about it."

"Let me look at it, stubborn man. I'm the one who loves you. It's my job." She leaned over to check his foot, rubbed the ankle and manipulated the joint. Nothing seemed broken. She continued the foot massage and watched him for reactions of pain.

He looked into her blue eyes and smiled. "I forgot what a soft touch you have."

"I haven't felt yours in a while either." She gave him a small pout.

"It's not right." TJ leaned in and kissed her forehead and lips. The second kiss lingered.

Willet smoothed back loose strands of her hair and gave him an intense look. "I want you."

"What?"

"I want you." She pressed him back and wrapped her arms around his neck. "I really do. I can't help it."

He pulled her closer, kissed her lips, nuzzled her neck. "I want you too," he murmured. "You mean right now?"

She kissed his chin and licked at the hollow of his throat, tasting salt. "Yes. I need you right now. Now. No, that can't be, we're in a dangerous place. What's wrong with me?"

He pressed his lips to hers, his tongue in her mouth, his kisses yearning and hungry. "I feel like I'm starving for you. We shouldn't, like you said, but…"

"Yes, we have to stop…" She leaned into his chest, circled his waist with her arms while he kissed her neck. It was quiet. They were alone. "We're out in the open…" They stripped off the vests they were wearing.

"Where's a good hotel when you need one?" He groaned as his hands found their way under her shirt. "Your skin feels like silk," he whispered. "I can't help it, Will. I need you now."

She gasped when his hands slid over her breasts. "Someone might see us," she murmured. "Don't stop."

He swung her back against the wall and pressed himself against her, pawing at her clothes, his breath ragged. She unzipped his pants. He lifted her onto his hips, and she wrapped her legs around him. He pinned her to the wall, not trying to be gentle. Her hips met his and an urgent moan escaped her. Lost in the moment, at the doorstep of the Underworld, they rocked together. Nothing else mattered until they both reached an aching climax that left them panting. They held on to each other and tried to catch their breath, Then, they remembered where they were.

TJ gently lowered her to the ground. "I'm sorry, Will," he said, looking into her eyes. "This place is not worthy of you."

"What do you mean?" She took a long, languorous stretch. "It was glorious!"

"It was that, but you deserve a nice bed, clean sheets, and champagne, not this filthy street. Did Red Souls do a fly-by and plant those thoughts in us? Were we hijacked?"

"I didn't hear them, but the whole city is saturated with Jat's influence."

They fumbled back into their clothes, tucking in shirts and arranging themselves into a semblance of order. TJ was still mumbling. "We're the Circle," he said, pulling up his pants. "We should have more self-control. Are we that helpless that we can't resist doing it in the street?"

Her smile turned mischievous. "Red Souls nudge us into things we'd like to do if our good sense didn't prevent it. If they made suggestions just now, we totally fell for them, because it was something we wanted to do anyway. I can't say it's the worst they ever did to me."

"We didn't do anything wrong, not really. Lucky they didn't tell us to kill somebody."

"Killing isn't in our nature, Thomas. Making love is. Red Souls tried to push us in our most susceptible direction. We didn't need much of a push to do what we did."

"Red Soul influence is not required," he groused buckling his belt, "but I prefer to ravish you on my own initiative."

Willet watched quietly. "Thomas, do you regret meeting me? I feel like all I've done is screw up your life and drag you into danger. It's not fair. Maybe there's another woman somewhere that would be easier to be with."

He wrapped his arms around her and laid his cheek on her hair. "Will, I've known a few women in my life, not that I'd boast. No one holds a candle to you. You're amazing and unique and incredibly brave, not to mention beautiful and sexy. Honestly, I can barely remember anyone else. You changed my life in weird and incomprehensible ways, but I wouldn't trade a moment of the craziness if it meant not being with you. I love you."

She took in these words, looked for the truth of them in his eyes, and found what she was looking for. "I love you too," she said, hugging him with all her strength. "I love you."

Time stood still in the depth of their embrace, a moment of peace and happiness but all too short. She twisted suddenly in his arms to look around. "Did you hear that? Voices. Someone's close, almost right next to us."

"Where? I don't see anyone."

"Voices, and another noise, I don't know what it is." Willet turned her head side to side, listening intently. "Sounds like gravel hitting the ground. People are talking." She blinked her eyes a few times. "Do things look blurry to you?"

The street shifted in and out of focus like frames of a movie speeding up and slowing down. Willet and TJ were alone, and then, between one blink and the next, there were people standing in front of the Dragon Head Building just a few feet away. It looked like a watery hologram of a group of men with shovels digging a hole in the front wall of the building. The sound of boots pounding on pavement came from the other direction, and another blurred hologram, five men in black uniforms approaching. It was a contingent of the Mayor's Guard with trumpet-shaped guns on their shoulders. They were coming on so fast, it seemed like everyone might collide right there in front of the Dragon Head Building. TJ and Willet quickly slipped on their vests to protect themselves from the mind-altering guns and pressed back against the wall. "Look out!" TJ called to the men digging. "You'll get shot!" If the men heard him, they didn't react.

The guards passed by TJ and Willet as if they were invisible and walked up to the front door of the building. They didn't give so much as a nod to the men digging into the wall. One guard waved a hand at the front door. It opened, and all five of them walked inside. The door closed behind them. No reaction from the diggers.

"What just happened?" TJ whispered. "This is too weird."

"I think we're on different time tracks, and the tracks are parallel," Willet said. "The soldiers, the diggers and us. We can see them, but they can't see us. We won't all be fully aware of each other until the tracks merge. I could hear them, so that was a heads-up. We must look like blurs too, and they're too busy to notice.

"Well, now we know guards are inside the building. Good intel."

The hologram-like image of the men digging into the wall came into focus, and then they were all standing on the street together. "Hey," TJ called to them. "Who are you?"

A man holding some kind of blower spun in the direction of TJ's voice and lifted the helmet he was wearing. "Where did you come from?" he said. "How'd you sneak up on us?"

"We were very quiet," Willet said. "And you were busy digging." Then she recognized him. "OH. Hi Bart."

Bart recognized her too. "Willet! It's you! And TJ. Finally! We've been waiting for you."

The other men raised shovels and tools, preparing to defend themselves, but Bart waved them back. "These are friends of Dean and Audrey. They're on the same mission we are. Where did you guys come from? Where's Audrey?"

"Audrey and Dean are on top of this building," Willet said, pointing up. "How did you end up here anyway?"

"A man at Griffith Park told me Audrey and Dean would be here. I have a load of crystal to deliver to them."

TJ eyed the small piles of crystal on the ground and the bags the men were holding. "I thought we nuked all the crystal in L.A. Where did you get so much?"

"I grew it from some chips that Audrey gave me. Arhat said it would help you guys."

"If Arhat said it would help, then it will," Willet agreed. "Did he say how to use it?"

"No, but it does eat through stone," Bart said. "We're using it to tunnel through this wall."

Rollie Zeemer stopped digging and wiped the sweat off his forehead with his sleeve. "A tall guy in a black suit just kidnapped Nick Hardman and the boy, Jonah, from the truck. We tried to stop him, but he turned into a cloud and blew right through us! Can you believe it? He disappeared right through the doors into the building. We can't get in the door, so we're digging in."

"Jonah's in there?" TJ groaned. "Sorry to tell you this, but the guy in the suit was Jat, the Deceiver. Nick and Jonah are in serious trouble. We have to get them out before this city disappears into the Underworld."

Yeah," Rollie said, "the guy in black introduced himself. That's why we're digging this hole."

"Jonah isn't the only kid in there," Edgar said. "My son, Robbie, is in there too. Do you have any suggestions? I'm beyond desperate."

"Not sure what to do about Jat, but it's likely there's a deranged man named Matt Gregg inside the building," TJ said. "Jat uses him like a puppet to do his dirty work. I can make him focus on me, because he hates my guts, but that might help everyone else to escape."

Edgar went back to digging frantically at the hole in the wall. Progress had been made. More stone had turned soft and loose as the crystal ate away at it. The hole was now bigger than a bowling ball. A person might soon be able to squeeze through.

"See," Bart said, "The crystal is working. Pretty soon we'll have a man-sized hole."

TJ and Willet looked at each other. Insight dawned on both of them. "This is better than dynamite, Will!" TJ said, grasping her shoulders. "No need to blow anything up. We'll use the crystal to weaken the foundation, and Audrey's rings will shake it loose. The building will drop, just like we planned. Perfect!"

"You intend to drop this building?" Major Tomasek said. "We need to be in and out before that happens."

"Like my apartment building," Jain said. "It fell flat as a pancake."

"We have to get in quick, find the boys and Nick, grab 'em and get out," TJ said in a take-charge manner. "Hold off on any more crystal than is needed to make the hole. When Jonah and Robbie are out and the building is cleared, we can load the perimeter with crystal. We'll need Audrey and Dean to finish the drop."

Edgar Zeemer gave TJ a hard look, but then he and Chuck Tomasek prepared to enter the building. TJ would lead the way since he had been inside it before. Jain insisted on going in to rescue Nick. They loaded up with ropes, repel hooks, light sticks and knives provisioned from the caravan trucks. Rollie and Bart kept digging until the hole was large enough for a man to squeeze through. TJ crawled inside. Edgar and Tomasek followed him, and Jain crawled in last. Bart and Rollie stood guard at the entrance.

That left Willet standing outside with Fire Chief Duggins, who eyed her with suspicion. "Who are you people?" the Chief demanded. "How did you get here without us noticing? There was nobody around, and then you were just - there."

Willet didn't want to spook him, but the truth would sound crazy no matter how she phrased it, so she decided to just spit it out. "We were on different tracks in time. Our time track collided with your time track, to put it simply. We're all on the same track now. Sorry, it sounds weird."

"That's absurd."

"It is what it is."

What are we supposed to do now?"

"If I go into a contemplation, can you keep an eye on my physical body?"

The Chief gave her a puzzled stare. "Ma'am, I'm a fire fighter, not a bodyguard," he said. "What do you think is gonna happen to your body?"

"I could get run over by a truck, or the guy in the black suit could come back."

"Whoa, whoa." Chief Duggins shook his head. "I can't help you with him. I still don't understand who that guy is."

"I get that. It's a lot for anyone to take in, but I have things to do that can't wait. Whatever you could do to protect me while I'm out would be appreciated." Willet sat cross-legged on the ground, took a deep breath and closed her eyes.

He sat down beside her. "What are you doing?"

"I'm going to sing 'HU'," she said.
 "What's a 'HU'?"

"HU is the song of the Soul. It helps me to move out beyond the physical in a body of light. My conscious self will separate from my physical body and leave it behind. This body may be vulnerable while I'm gone."

"Separate from your body? That's death."

"No, just movement into another state of consciousness."

He stared at her.

Willet took another deep breath and a slow exhale. "I need to help TJ find the boys and Nick. I can't do it sitting here, and I can't just walk into the building, so I'm going to use a body that moves faster, sees clearer and hears even better than I can physically."

"That's nuts," he said. "Totally nuts."

"It's a different world inside the building, Chief Duggins. Another rate of vibration. Different senses are needed to see and hear in there. I have them."

He gave her a hard stare. "Never heard of such a thing. Sounds unnatural."

"It's totally natural."

"If it's so natural, why do you need protection?"

"Like I said, I'll be gone from here. Please just trust me and help me. Watch over this body." She had no more time for explanations. She closed her eyes and began singing 'HU' in a single long, soft note.

The Chief watched her relax, her face serene. The chant sounded nice. He might try it some time, but right now he had to protect the body in front of him. Shifting shadows moved in corners around nearby buildings, shafts of light cut through the air at odd angles and then disappeared. Cold chills ran over his skin. He thought he heard whispers. "You're hallucinating again, Clancy," he murmured to himself. "When this is over, take your pension and retire like the wife wants you to, before you lose your mind completely."

He looked over his shoulder to where Rollie and Bart were digging. If the tall man in the black suit tried to carry him and the woman into that building, he'd need some backup. Shadows were spreading out and creeping closer to where he and Willet sat in the street. What caused shadows when there wasn't any sun? And that odd clicking sound. He began to sweat. He was ready to pick the woman up and make a run for it.

Chapter 11

The sight of the lobby inside the Dragon Head Building made TJ remember things he did not want to remember - fighting for his life with sharp needles in his muscles, the painful journey through the laser room with burns all over his body. Only the thought of Jonah trapped in the building kept him going through that trial. He had to stop and take a deep breath, or risk turning around and running back out to the street, but he couldn't do that. Jonah was trapped in here. Again. TJ had to get him out.

"What's up, son?" Major Tomasek asked TJ. "You went pale as a ghost." The Marine looked hard as nails and unfamiliar with the word 'fear'. A good man to have on their team.

TJ pulled himself together and brought everyone up to speed on the dangers they faced. "This building is full of really bad things, let's get that straight right now," he said, looking particularly at Edgar. "And it's eighty-nine stories high. We'll try the elevator, which may or may not stop on the floors we want. When the elevator doors open, be prepared for anything, and I mean anything, on the other side. We're not in the same world we were in outside. Remember, we're here to find the boys and Nick and get them out. Let's not get distracted."

"This building is empty," said Edgar. "A little dark, maybe. I don't see a problem."

"There's nothing regular about this building."

"How do we search eighty-nine floors?" Jain asked. "That's a lot of places to hide bodies."

"Willet will help us. We call her 'the Listener'. She'll provide surveillance and communications, listen for sounds of life and let me know where to look. That'll cut down our search time." TJ sounded more certain than he felt. There was so much that could go wrong.

The men looked at him like he was crazy. "That young woman we left outside is our comms and intel?" Major Tomasek snorted. "Tell me you're kidding."

"Willet has skills. I don't have time for a full explanation, so you'll have to trust me. Let's just find Nick and the boys and get out of here. They're probably freaked by now."

The team plotted their next moves. There weren't many to choose from. "We'll go straight to the top floor," TJ said. "That's Matt Gregg's office. If he's there, he'll know where the boys are. He'll try to stop us, so, let's get it over with."

"What about all the other floors?" Edgar said, pointing to the numbered buttons on the panel. "My boy could be on one of them. I want to check them in case he's there."

"Let's start with the most likely floors, Edgar. I know you're anxious, but I have reason to believe the boys are on the eighty-ninth. I was up there before. Like I said, trust me on this."

"Trust you?" Edgar said. "I don't even know you! Robbie is in trouble. He could be injured. I can't just wait to get all the way to the top floor." Edgar's face was sweaty, and his eyes were wild. Distress over his son was beginning to overcome his good sense.

"Edgar. We'll find him."

"Did you get some kind of, uh, intel?" Tomasek chortled. "Did your lady whisper in your ear?"

"Not yet, but you can count on it."

Willet's point of view moved through the tunnel of light that began in her Third Eye, leaving the Fire Chief and the street behind. Her light body came out at the other end with a soft pop. As wonderful as it felt to be free of the physical shell, she couldn't linger. There was a job to do. Her light body moved effortlessly through the wall of the Dragon Head Building to the inside of the ground floor. The core of the building looked completely different than it did the last time she saw it. There was no lobby. Fog filled the central space, swirling and shifting, thick as primordial protoplasm. She heard the crack of lightning high above. Voices echoed from different directions. She floated up to about the fourth floor where Mayor's Guards stood on a platform outside the elevator door with guns raised, as if waiting for someone to step out. She had to warn TJ. She listened for his heartbeat and breath, sounds she'd recognize anywhere. TJ was in the elevator with the other men. First floor. She propelled herself with swimming motions and reached the first floor elevator. She moved through the doors and felt the cold metal mingle with the atoms of her light body. In the elevator, TJ and the men were arguing. She had to get his attention.

"TJ!" she whispered, "Listen to me."

TJ's head swung in her direction. He nodded slightly.

"Guards on the fourth floor. Don't stop there."

"Understood," he murmured.

She floated back out to the center space and up to the top floor. It was full of spider webs. An overwhelming sense of terror hit her. There were heartbeats, some fluttering, some pounding. She didn't see anyone. She rose higher, above all the webs, and saw a spider hanging by a thread. Lady G. was sleeping. The heartbeats she heard were coming from the webs. Somewhere, inside that maze, the young boys and Nick were trapped. She thought of TJ, and her light body immediately streaked down the elevator shaft until she was beside him in the elevator.

"Heartbeats on the top floor," she whispered. "The boys and Nick are there. The spider is up there too. Be very quiet. Do you understand?"

He nodded again.

"Don't wake her."

The elevator continued its rise, and Willet moved out of the elevator into the core of the building. The miasmic fog in the center of the building was compressing, taking on a shape. She pressed herself against a wall to avoid getting caught in it. A form flickered in and out of sight, both there and not there. A mouth with a flicking serpent tongue appeared, then shoulders and an arm. Then a giant man was standing on the ground, very long legs with lizard feet, toes spread out. He was at least twenty feet tall and wore a black suit. Long arms ended in enormous hands with taloned fingers. The man probed the corners and crevices of the building with his talons, searching for something. It was Jat, and her presence distracted him. His eyes burned as he searched for her. Long black hair floated around his head. He smelled of rotting things, of death. Even in her light body, it nauseated her.

"Lissstener," Jat hissed. "You are a spy in my house. Get out."

His jaw dropped opened, revealing a cavernous mouth rimmed with square black teeth. A sound loud as an air horn blared out of his throat. It was the loudest, most deafening sonic assault Willet had ever experienced. Stars danced in front of her eyes, and a spike of pain lanced through her. The power behind the sound sent her into freefall. She hit the ground floor, lost connection with her light body, and slammed back into her physical body like a cannonball.

*****

Chief Duggins was already on edge, but he jumped straight up when Willet's body shuddered and keeled over. Dark liquid flowed from her ears and dripped onto the sidewalk. In the low light, it had little color, but Duggins could smell it. Blood. He shook off his own shock, slipped his jacket off and folded it under her head, pressing it against her ears. With trembling hands, he checked her vital signs as he was trained to do. Her pulse was weak, and her breathing was almost undetectable. He administered mouth-to-mouth. Nothing changed. He was losing her. Gripped by panic, he called out for help to anyone who could hear him.

A brown-skinned woman with tight brown curls burnished gold, wearing a long maroon skirt and white ruffled peasant blouse, suddenly stood beside him. A large black dog with a white star on its forehead stood at her side. Duggins never heard them approach.

The woman dropped to one knee and took Willet's hand. "Listener," she said. "Come back to us. It is not your time." She began to sing that same HU chant that Willet had been singing, in a long, low tone on a single breath. The dog dropped down on its haunches and laid her head on Willet's stomach.

Duggins felt helpless watching for signs of life to return. He stole a glance at the woman kneeling beside the girl. She hummed that HU word softly. Not knowing what else to do, he hummed along with her. His breathing got easier as moments went by. Soothing light glowed behind his eyes and flowed through his limbs like warm honey. The woman, the dog and the girl were enveloped in the same light.

Willet's eyelids fluttered. She opened her eyes and gave them a blank stare.

"Baby girl," said the woman softly, stroking her hand. "What happened? Are you in pain? Where are the others?"

"Gem," Willet whispered, "I can't hear what you're saying. I'm deaf."

Chapter 12

The Traveler took Audrey to the eighty-seventh floor of the Dragon Head Building where she stepped out of a space-time fold into a dark stairwell. A metal stairway anchored to the wall rose to a door on the next higher level. Audrey walked to the stairs. "What are we doing here?" she asked.

"Be careful of the eighty-nineth floor," Sonrisa told her. "I advise against stepping out directly on that floor. You can begin here and then climb the next two flights by stair. Enter the top floor very quietly."

That sounded like good advice. "Are you coming too?" Audrey asked.

"This fight must be yours," Sonrisa replied. "You are needed here. The Guardian will join you soon. Meanwhile, keep your wits about you and maintain your focus. This building is full of traps."

With those words of guidance, Sonrisa disappeared into spacetime, leaving Audrey alone in the stairwell. The thought of what she might find up the stairs filled her with cold dread. She shivered and her insides quaked. When Gem or Sonrisa was with her, she had confidence. She rode in the wake of their power and purpose, but she didn't feel so confident now. She climbed the last flight of stairs with footsteps as quiet as she could step, whispering the HU chant under her breath to calm her pounding heart. She paused to listen, wishing she had her sister's incredible hearing, but the silence revealed nothing. At the top of the stairs, there was a large black metal door. She reached for the chrome handle and eased the door open, hoping it wouldn't squeak. A dark hallway led to a second door with a crack of light showing at the floor. She walked to that door and opened it as quietly as she could and entered a large room with rafters and high windows that were streaked and dirty. The room felt warm and clammy. Fine white dust floated in the air, and a maze of white threads crisscrossed the room from wall to wall. Spider webs. This claustrophobic space had to be the spider's lair. Her stomach twisted at the putrid smell of something decomposing hit her nose. She shuddered at the thought of what might cause that awful smell.

A familiar voice spoke softly near her ear. "Auddie, stay quiet, the spider is sleeping," her sister's voice said. "Look up."

Audrey looked up. There was Black Widow Barbie, suspended by a single thread from a beam high in the ceiling. The spider hung upside down, long legs folded up onto her body. Spiders sleep regularly to restore their energy. While the spider slept, Audrey might have time to do what she came to do – rescue Dean and get him out before the spider stirred.

She reached out to one of the strands of the web and gave it a light touch. It was made of a fiber like silk, stronger than it looked, and sticky. When it wrapped around a body, it was impossible for a body to escape. The spider's prey would inevitably become food. She remembered her dream of having such strands wrapped tight around her own body. That thought caused three rings to spin up on the fingers of each hand and heat quickly. She moved forward into the maze, letting the hot rings cut through the threads like circular blades. She peered through the maze of white, searching for anything that might be trapped in it. Sure enough, shadowed bundles wrapped in silk hung in the web. One of the bundles might be Dean. A spider sprays its prey with digestive fluid from tubes on either side of its mouth and saves it for later. By the time the spider begins to eat, it can suck the food into its mouth like soup. Her heart jumped into her throat at the gruesome image. *Please Dean please. Don't be food.*

The cuts on her arm from fighting Matt Gregg were sore and inflamed. The arm felt so heavy, she could hardly lift it, but she put the pain out of her mind and let her rings spin hotter, holding them out, and slowly, carefully, melted the web, clearing it away with sweeps of her hands until she reached the first bundle. It was the size of a full-grown man hanging at her eye level. She ran her hands around the bundle, melting the threads that held it suspended and eased it down to the floor. She cut carefully through the sticky web wrapping and peeled it back. It was a male, someone she didn't recognize. His eyes popped open with a look of pure terror. She freed his head from the web, then the rest of his body. He smelled bad, having lost control of both bladder and bowels. Audrey eased him to the floor and put a finger to her lips to silence him, then gestured for him to go to the elevator and sit down, stay put. The spider still hung motionless by its thread. So far so good, but she hadn't found Dean.

She moved on to the next bundle and cut it out of the web, peeled back the threads wrapped around the head. It was Nick Hardman. "Nick," Audrey whispered, patting his cheek. She pulled the spider's silk wrapping away from his body. Nick Hardman, retired Army, rolled out of the bundle onto the floor. He didn't move, didn't open his eyes. His skin was gray, and his lips were blue. She put a finger under his nose. No breath. *Dead.* He didn't look eaten. It could have been heart attack or asphyxiation. She should have been prepared for this, but she wasn't. A hard lump formed in her throat.

 "I'm so sorry Nick," she whispered. "I should have killed that spider when I had the chance. I didn't realize how evil she was."

Another person she knew died on her watch. It was more death than she'd ever experienced. Her mind raced as she tried to think of what she could do for Nick, but there was nothing. She had to leave him where he lay for the time being and try to keep the spider from eating him. She could try to prevent that indignity at least.

She moved on, swiping through the web with her rings and melting it until she reached the next bundle. It was smaller than the first two. She cut quickly to release it from the web and brought it to the floor, sliced through the sides of the tight wrap and peeled back the silk. A boy's lifeless form emerged. He seemed to be about eleven years old. His damp clothes clung to his skin, and his checks were streaked with dried tears. *Please don't be dead. Please don't be dead.* She checked for signs of life. *Breathing, thank goodness.* She didn't know this boy, but it didn't matter. He had to be saved. She tried to rouse him with light pats under his chin. His eyes opened, and he stared at her in a daze. She raised her finger to her lips, locked on his eyes until she got a glimmer of understanding, and then shook her head slowly. He could not under any circumstances make a sound. New tears welled in the boy's eyes, and his lips trembled. To his credit, he didn't bawl out loud. She raised him to his feet and supported his arm. He wobbled unsteadily. She led him to the corner by the elevator and motioned him to sit. He slid down against the wall with his knees to his chest. Silent tears shook his body.

On to the next bundle, also boy-sized, and cut it down. It was Jonah. His eyes were steady when she freed his head from the wrap, but his breathing was rapid. She gave him the sign for quiet. With visible effort he calmed his breath. What a trooper. She helped him to stand and led him to the elevator. Jonah sat next to the other boy, and she went back to work. The next bundle looked oddly shaped. She couldn't quite analyze why until she got closer. It was a man, partially unwrapped, with his head half-eaten. One bloodshot hazel eye stared at her from the intact side of the head. For the second time in five minutes, she had the urge to vomit violently. That would be noisy and smelly. It might wake the spider. Fortunately, there was nothing in her stomach, but the sight of that eye would be stamped into her memory for the rest of her life, another souvenir of the battle for L.A.

Where is Dean?
Her chest swelled painfully with panic. If she found him half-eaten, she would not be able to handle it.

She moved faster, swinging her arms and hands to cut through the webs. There were three more bundles she could see, and they all had to be freed. She reached the first bundle and cut it out of the web. It was a woman, blue-skinned, and dead. Audrey laid her down as gently as she could and moved on. The next bundle was a man, also dead. His neck was ravaged and bloody. Lady G had already started to chew on him, then stopped for some reason. Maybe just a snack? Who knew the logic of an evil and demented arachnid? She made her way to the last bundle hanging higher in the web. *Please be Dean.* She stretched up on her toes to cut through the threads. The bundle sagged out of the web. She eased it down to the floor. "Dean," she whispered. "Can you hear me?" She was afraid to open it, afraid of what she might find, but she felt for the head and cut away the wrapping. Dean's brown hair emerged, then his face. He looked pale and his eyes were closed. She put her hands on his cheeks. They were warm, a welcome sign of life. She finished cutting the wrapping away from his body and quickly checked him for injuries. He looked rumpled and damp, and there was blood on his hands, but no parts of him looked chewed. She laid down beside him and put her arm over his chest.

After a couple of seconds, his chest rose in a breath. *Thank you. Thank you, Lord.* "Dean," she whispered in his ear. "Please wake up. It's me. We gotta get out of here."

*****

"There are guards on the fourth floor," TJ told the other men. "The boys and Nick are on the top floor We have to go there first and not waste time on the other floors."

Edgar seemed ready to snap. "What if you're wrong?" he growled. "I don't like skipping floors. I told you that. We might miss Robbie. If anything happens to him, I will hold you personally responsible."

"There's no harm in starting at the top floor, Ed," Tomasek said reasonably. "Then we can backtrack our way down and check the other floors. We'll find your boy."

They got on the elevator, TJ pushed the button for the eighty-nineth floor, and they began to rise. After a minute, Edgar made a quick reach around TJ and hit the open-door button on the panel. TJ quickly hit the close button and turned on Edgar. "Are you nuts?"

"I said I want to search every floor!"

"There are eighty-nine floors! It'll take too long. And besides, I already know where they are!"

"Says you!" Edgar lunged at TJ.

They traded shoves, both reaching for the button panel. The elevator stopped abruptly at the fourth floor, just where Willet told TJ they shouldn't go. The doors slid open, and five Mayor's Guards were standing there with guns pointed and at the ready.

Tomasek reacted with the speed of a trained U.S. Marine and snapped his heavy rope at them, sending two Guards sprawling backwards and jostling the others. A few precious seconds were gained. Jain dropped to the floor, raised the stun gun he had and fired into the faces of the Guards still standing. The gun blast must have touched some patch of skin despite the Guards helmets and goggles, because the three Guards swayed on their feet. The trumpet-shaped barrels of their guns tilted toward the floor, and then the guns slipped out of their hands.

TJ pounded on the close-door button. The elevator doors slid shut, and they began to climb. He grabbed Edgar by the shirt and got in his face. "If those Guards shoot us, we'll never make it out of here, let alone rescue anyone else. There are as many ways to get permanently lost in this building as there are floors. Do you hear me? Are my words penetrating your thick skull?"

Edgar pushed him off hard and straightened his shirt. "If you touch me like that again, *I'll* kill you. Just because you want to find some kid, doesn't mean you know what it's like to have a son trapped in here. If you did, you'd understand. You'd stop at nothing to find him."

TJ closed his eyes a moment and took a deep breath. "I *will* stop at nothing. There are people in here I care about too, and I'll do whatever it takes to save them. I know where the boys are. They're on the top floor. I'm trying to help you, but you have to let me."

Edgar gave him a killing glare and a raised fist. "Says who, your ghost girlfriend?" He was shorter than TJ, but he had heft and his fists looked hard as rock. The temperature rose in the small space. TJ raised his own fists, and Jain stepped back into a corner.

Tomasek got between Edgar and TJ and extended an arm at each of them. "Whoa Ed, let's take it down a notch. Fighting each other will only slow us down."

Edgar threw a punch in the direction of TJ's face and managed to hit Tomasek in the ear. The Marine major grabbed Edgar's arm and flipped him on his behind with practiced ease. "Can we move on now?" he said calmly.

The elevator developed a mind of its own after that. It stopped every second or third floor, and the doors opened randomly on the empty core of the building. Voices echoed through the hollowed-out interior from too far away to decipher words, but the cries and wails were clear enough.

It was driving Edgar crazy. "What is that?" he said. He was on edge already, and the sounds amped him even higher. "Someone is crying. Could be Robbie. I have to find him!" The doors slammed shut in his face, and the elevator resumed its erratic climb. A few floors higher, and the doors opened again. The cries were louder now and more distressed. Edgar was losing his mind and wanted to jump out, but there was only empty space outside the elevator doors. They slid closed, and the elevator rose.

"It's going too slow!" he yelled and pounded his fists on the doors. "I gotta get outta here!" He made a quick poke at the button panel and stopped the elevator. When the doors opened this time, the distinct cries of a young boy echoed through the empty interior. "Dad! Dad! Help!" Edgar launched himself at the open doors, his chest thrust out into open space. He was ready to jump out into a freefall.

TJ and Tomasek grabbed his arms, and Jain wrapped his arms around Edgar's waist to drag him back. Edgar tried to throw them off. "Robbie's out there! Lemme go!" The doors closed. The rise of the elevator continued in an excruciatingly slow series of stops and starts. Sometimes the doors opened, sometimes they didn't. The control panel lit up at each floor - twenty-seven, thirty, thirty-six, forty. They were sitting on Edgar to keep him from bolting every time the doors opened. It was like subduing a mad bull.

"There's nothing out there, Edgar," TJ gritted out through his teeth as he pushed the man's struggling shoulders to the floor. "You'll only fall to your death."

Edgar bucked like a bronco. His robust physique gave him a lot of leverage, but they kept him pinned. The elevator lurched to another stop at the forty-third floor. When the doors slid open, the doorway was filled by black silky fabric with a large black button in a buttonhole. Everyone stared, trying to figure out what they were seeing.

"It's the black suit," Jain said finally, his voice quivering. "It's *him*, the guy who took Nick. Let me at him!"

TJ had to jump off Edgar and hold Jain back until the doors closed. "Get a hold of yourselves," Tomasek growled, "before you get us all killed." Jain scowled and leaned back against the back of the elevator. Edgar continued to struggle.

"OK," TJ said. "Now we know Jat's out there. Under no circumstances can you approach these doors again before the eighty-nineth floor. We will find Robbie and Jonah there. Just stay cool and keep it together."

At the fifty-sixth floor, Edgar managed a reach-around and hit the open-door button again. A huge eye peered in through the doors. Its shiny black surface reflected their startled faces, and red flames burned in the depths of its pupil. A long black-taloned finger slid into the elevator, poked and probed, and tried to scoop them out like bugs from a hollow log. The men scrambled up against the slippery walls, yelling and trying to reach the ceiling, but there was nothing to grab on to. Tomasek fell on top of the leather-skinned digit with his knife and stabbed at it repeatedly with all his strength. It was like stabbing rhinoceros hide with a toothpick.

TJ jammed on the button to close the doors. They slid together and banged against the finger over and over. The finger wiggled and pulled out. The doors finally shut, and the elevator resumed its climb. TJ turned on Edgar and the others, white-faced and furious. "Do you understand what I'm telling you now? This building is cursed! He knows we're in here, and he will stop at nothing to get at us. Our only chance is to make it to the eighty-nineth floor before he rips the elevator apart. Don't argue with me." This time, nobody did.

They finally reached the top floor, the elevator doors opened, and they stepped out into the dense maze of white threads that filled the room. The maze distorted the light coming from high windows, and the smell was horrid.

"Something's dead in here," Tomasek mumbled. "I'd know that smell anywhere."

Jonah and Robbie were sitting in the corner where Audrey had left them. Edgar shouted "Robbie!" and ran to his son, gathered the boy to his chest. Father and son sobbed. "Are you alright, son? Are you hurt?" Robbie didn't speak. He just held on to his father and shook his head. "How about you, boy? Are you OK?" Edgar said to Jonah. Jonah shrugged.

Tomasek walked over and crouched down in front of the boys. "What happened to you?" He got silent stares from both boys. He checked their pulses, felt their foreheads for fever, and looked closely into their eyes.

"They're in shock," he said. 'They're pupils are constricted, and their skin is cold. We have to get them warm and hydrated." Tomasek gave Edgar a narrow stare. "Can you take the elevator down to the ground floor without pitching a fit? Keep your cool. Don't open the doors 'til you get to the bottom."

Edgar returned the stare. "This is my son. Do you really think I'd do something to put him in danger? We're leaving." He ushered the boys into the elevator and made room for the frightened man who had soiled himself.

"Edgar?" TJ added. "Send the elevator back up here after you reach the ground. We'll need it."

Edgar gave him an unpleasant smirk. The doors closed, and the elevator dropped.

*****

Audrey heard the elevator doors bump open and footsteps
shuffle, after which a man's voice cried 'Robbie'. Her quiet
advantage was over at that point. A high-pitched keening
squeal broke from above. Lady G had awakened and was
spinning on her thread like a crazed acrobat, long legs
unfolding as she flipped over. White thread reeled out of the
spinneret on her abdomen and dropped her onto the web. She
scuttled into the maze of white thread and disappeared.
Audrey heated two rings and positioned herself next to Dean,
waiting for the spider to attack. As soon as the spider's form
appeared through the maze, she let fly a hot ring that hit the
spider hard in the left eye. The eye sizzled and crumbled to
dust. "That's for killing Nick, you filthy bug," Audrey said
through her teeth. She threw a second ring, managed to hit a
long, spindly leg and sliced it in two.

The spider gave a high keening screech of fury but was not
slowed by either injury. She came scampering over the
threads, swift on her remaining legs, and suddenly appeared
on the other side of Dean, touching his body with her front
legs. It looked like she was about to mount him.

"No!" Audrey shouted. She threw all the rings on her fingers at once. "Stay back, or I'll dissect you."

The spider shook off the ring barrage but came to a stop. A clicking sound came from between its fangs, and then the scathing voice of Lady G emerged from the spider's mouth in a word loaded with contempt. "You." Fluid dripped off her fangs. "I am so sick of *you!*" she shrieked, loud enough that her words echoed off the rafters." My web is damaged, and my food is scattered. I will eat your brain. You will be alive while I do it."

"I'll cut you in half," Audrey spat, matching the spider's menace. "Your pal, the Lizard Mayor, already lost his head. What body part do you want to lose first?"

The rings were spinning hot and fast on her fingers. She let one ring fly, aiming for the spider's body. It grazed the underbelly and left a long, flaming scar, but it didn't stop the spider.

Lady G jumped at Audrey, knocked her to the ground and landed on top of her, their faces inches apart. "Your silly rings cannot stop me. I have feasted on this earth for time beyond memory. I am legend." An ugly laugh came from her mouth. "The Great Jat promised if I tasted the brain of one of the Guardian's Circle, he would gift me with children. I will have many offspring. They will overrun this pathetic city."

Audrey was pinned under the spider's abdomen, no room to use rings without burning herself. She pushed against the hard shell, trying to make enough space to roll free. "You don't seem like the maternal type, Georgina. Don't spider babies eat their mother after they hatch?"

Audrey felt white sticky thread spread over her arms. Her dream of being trapped in a web became a living nightmare. If the spider wrapped her completely, it was game over. She freed her left hand and flipped a small ring at the spider's head, trying to distract her. The spider knocked it away with a long leg, earning a burnt foot for the trouble. Audrey managed a bigger ring with her right hand and was able to hook it onto one of the spider's crooked fangs, then grabbed the ring with both hands and yanked it down. The skin of her palms smoked.

The spider reared back like a bucking bronco, using the leverage of her large body, and jerked her head back. The sudden move sent Audrey flying over the spider's back into a mass of sticky webs. The struggle to free herself just got her more stuck, but she had to divert the spider's attention away from Dean. All she could do was shout. "Here I am! Come and get me."

Chapter 13

TJ and the men heard Audrey's voice in the back of the room
before they actually saw her. Her words were muffled, but the
tone was urgent. She was in a fight, and it wasn't going well.
Major Tomasek started cutting through the webs with his
pocketknife, but soon stuffed the knife back in his pocket,
grumbling. "The threads are too sticky to cut and stronger
than they look. We have to try something else."

TJ had a rope with a repelling hook at the end of it. He threw
it into the web and ripped away a bunch of the gossamer
threads. Another throw ripped even more.

Tomasek pumped his fist. "That's more like it."

Jain called out for Nick. "Nicky, where are you? I'm here,
dude! Talk to me."

The farther into the maze they went, the more bodies they found on the floor. Jain ran to each one until he found Nick. A shriek of anguish broke out of him. The sobs that followed left no doubt to anyone within hearing that Nick Hardman was dead. TJ and Tomasek came to his side. Tomasek checked for a pulse and then looked up at Jain and shook his head. The expression on Jain's face was pure pain. They helped him lift Nick's body and carry it to the elevator, where they laid him down carefully.

TJ didn't know Jain or Nick, but he knew grief when he saw it. "I'm sorry, man. Really sorry. This is a tragedy."

If Jain heard, he gave no sign. Tears welled in his eyes, and his mouth was a rigid grimace. "Someone's gonna pay," he snarled. He stalked off with hands curled into fists to find the killer. TJ and Tomasek followed him deeper into the maze of webs.

*****

Willet sat up suddenly, despite her bleeding ears. "Thomas is in danger! I need to get back in there!" The sudden movement and effort to speak made her head ache. She groaned, swaying dizzily.

"Your eardrums are blown," Chief Duggins said, easing her into a reclining position. "It happens to firefighters when something explodes in a fire. That's why we wear earplugs. How did this happen to you?"

She struggled up onto her elbows. "Jat made a deafening sound to disable me. He's looking for TJ, and something bad will happen if he finds him!" The effort was too much for her. She fell backward.

"Hold on there," Duggins said. He caught her before her head hit the ground and laid her gently down. "Punctured eardrums are painful. They'll affect your hearing for a while. Your balance won't be good either. You need to stay still."

"You don't understand!" Willet said, her voice weak. "I have to go back in there."

Gem knelt beside her and put a hand on her shoulder. She shook her head 'no'.

Willet saw the 'no' but wasn't having it. "There are people on the top floor, Gem! That's where the boys are. Jat turned into a giant, and his body fills the whole building. There's no place to hide from him." She laid down again and closed her eyes. She wasn't sure she could actually do anything. A pinpoint of light appeared in her Third Eye, and a buzzing sound tickled her left ear. She breathed in and out, let the sound of Huuuuu ride on her breath, and then she was floating above her physical body. Moments later, she was back inside the Dragon Head Building.

*****

The spider climbed on top of Dean and straddled him.

"Dean!" Audrey cried from the sticky threads that held her. "Punch her! Knock her off!"

 Wide awake now, Dean threw an uppercut fist that hit the spider in the head. "Get off me!" He tried to roll away.

The spider reared back in surprise and made that angry keening sound. Prey usually didn't fight back when they were caught in her web. She stepped on Dean's shoulders and leaned in with fangs snapping at his face. "Why do you fight me?" she said in a cajoling voice. "Humans are food for spiders. Accept it."

"Punch her again, Dean!" Audrey shouted. "Aim for the good eye!" She was able to cut herself out of the web with small rings in each hand burning through the threads. Finally free, she jumped down beside the spider.

Lady G didn't stop to look at her. Drops of fluid beaded on the tubes at either side of her mouth. Digestive fluid dripped on Dean's face. It would soften him, but she wouldn't wait for that. She'd eat him right away.

"Help us!" Audrey screamed when she saw TJ, Jain and Tomasek burst through the web." Get the bug off him!"

The men spun their hooked ropes like lassos over their heads. Tomasek's hook landed on the spider's body and embedded into her back. He planted his feet and pulled back hard. The spider fought to hold ground. TJ threw another hook into her back. They tried to drag the spider off of Dean, but Lady G used her remaining legs and the leverage of her big body to resist.

Audrey combined two rings into one that was large, hot and sharp-edged and hurled it edge-first toward the spider with all her strength. The ring sliced through the middle of the spider's body like a buzzsaw. Lady G was cut in two between the cephalothorax and abdomen. TJ and Tomasek yanked on the ropes. The abdomen broke away and the back half of her body fell over, back legs flailing. That should have been enough to stop her, but her front legs still worked and had Dean pinned. The spider doused Dean's body with digestive fluids. Acidic liquid hit the skin of his neck and burned into the epidermis. Dean wailed in pain and threw left and right hooks at her head as she leaned in to take a bite.

Jain climbed up on the front half of the spider's body and hammered at it with his fists, cracking into the carapace shell. "You bitch! This is for Nick!" He kept pounding until he smashed the cephalothorax to splinters. The only part of the spider still intact was the head. Jain reached around, grabbed one of the fangs and yanked it to the side. There was a crack behind the head, and the front legs collapsed. Jain slid to the ground and kicked what was left of the corpse over and over, cursing at it, until the bug was close to mush.

"Get it off me! Get it off me!" Dean yelled as he tried to shove of the spider's head away.

TJ and Audrey pushed the cephalothorax over and rolled it clear of Dean's body. Dean struggled to his knees and mopped digestive fluid off his face and neck with the sleeves of his shirt, then ripped the shirt off and used the inside to wipe away more of the fluid. His skin had turned a raw, bubbling red.

"We need water!" Audrey shouted. No one had any. She used her own shirt to help wipe his face. The corrosive fluid burned right through the cloth. Audrey heard a familiar voice.

"Move aside, please, Ring Thrower."

Gem and Dora stood behind her. Gem turned her Freezing Breath into a gush of ice water and showered Dean's head, face and neck until his clothes were drenched. The sudden cold stung.

Dean yelped, but as his skin cooled and the digestive fluid washed away, he sucked deep breaths and slowly calmed. "Oh, wow, that feels good," he said finally and touched light fingers to his face. "I'm almost numb." He laid down on the floor, curled into the fetal position, and shut his eyes.

Audrey kneeled beside him. She took his hand and kissed it, felt his forehead, and laid a gentle palm on his blistered cheek. His reddened skin looked so painful it brought tears to her eyes. "I tried to find you sooner," she said. "I should have prevented this." He mumbled something through swollen lips, but she couldn't make it out. "Can you stand up?" she asked. "I'll help you."

His voice broke, and his shoulders shook. "That thing was about to eat me! I was gonna be eaten by a spider. That happens movies, not real life."

A panicked mewling bubbled out of his throat like the sound of a child frightened by something so horrible that it was beyond his ability to comprehend. Deep, heaving gasps rocked his body. Audrey slid her arms under his and tried to lift him. He was too heavy for her to move, so she settled back down next to him and tried to comfort him with hugs and assurances of the spider's demise.

"It's over, Dean," she murmured. "The bug is dead."

Dean would not be comforted. "It'll never be over. Not for me. Her mouth was on my face. I smelled her breath."

Audrey's heart ached for him. "I was afraid I'd never see you again, but you're alive, I'm alive, and the spider is dead. We'e together! We can overcome everything else."

Dean buried his head in her neck. "Thank you. Thank you, babe," he said over and over. "You saved me."

Major Tomasek kneeled next to them and took inventory of Dean's injuries. Another shock victim, with first degree burns. "This is starting to feel like a war zone," he said. "Good thing I have med training. I think you'll recover, but you'll need to see a real doctor."

TJ came and sat down beside them. He patted Dean's shoulder and grasped his other hand. "Deano," he said quietly. "Sorry to say, we've got another situation to deal with downstairs. Jat's inside the building, gearing up for a big assault. The city's about to fall. Are you with us?"

"I don't have anything left," Dean said so softly they could barely hear him. "You'll have to fight without me. I'll stay here."

"That's not an option, buddy. We need you. This building must come down, and you can't be in it when it does. We can't bring it down without the full Circle. As for the acid burns on your face, we'll deal with it when we get back to normal. I know a great plastic surgeon. He'll do skin grafts. You'll be good as new."

"Don't care about my looks right now, if that's what you mean. I just want this nightmare to be over."

For a moment, they forgot Gem was there, but then they heard her voice. "Warrior. Do not let the Deceiver have the last word. The Circle must write the final narrative."

Dean rolled over on his back and groaned. "I don't know what that means, woman. What am I supposed to do?"

"The Deceiver has his foot on the neck of the city. We must break his leg. Stand up now."

Dean struggled to his feet and shook off his malaise. Then everything began to shake. There was a rumble deep in the bowls of the building like tumbling boulders. Moments later, an explosion blew a large hole through the floor, up through the roof, and into the sky, sending debris flying in every direction. They all scrambled to the corners of the room and covered their heads. The Deceiver was making his move.

"Major, it's time for you and Jain to leave," TJ called out. "It's not safe for you here."

"What about you?" Tomasek shouted. "It's not safe for you either. You're coming with us, right?"

"We have work to do here. The crystal is eating the foundation of the building, making it unstable. The Circle will apply the necessary pressure to shake it loose. You need to be gone as soon as possible before this whole structure falls. I can't guarantee how long you have before that happens."

"You people are scary nuts," Tomasek muttered, shaking his head, "I don't know what you're doing, but we're out of here. Give us as much time as you can, huh? It's a long way to the ground floor if we have to take the stairs."

"Thank you, gentleman," Audrey added. "If it wasn't for you, that spider would have devoured us."

Tomasek and Jain dropped low on hands and knees and crawled along the walls to the elevator where Nick Hardman's body still lay. In moments, a bell rang. The elevator doors slid open, then shut. That left the Circle staring at the hole in the floor. They edged over to it and took a look down.

Jat stood below in the core of the building. He was almost as tall as the building itself, and his head was enormous. He looked up at them. A smirk played on his lips, and flames burned in his eyes. "Shall we end this little charade now?" he chided as he smiled. "Surely you are as tired of the game as I am. If you give up quietly, I will let you have the city to rule as your own, your very own kingdom in the Underworld. You may reign with a free hand. That sounds nice, does it not?"

Gem formed an ice ball between her hands and threw it at him. The Guardian had good aim. The ice ball hit Jat in the forehead. He actually flinched, and the smirk on his lips twisted into a nasty grimace. He showed them a mouthful of square black teeth. "If that is your answer, the alternative I offer is not as pleasant. You will experience your own decay and death, the dismal end of your physical existence."

"The Circle does not bargain with the Deceiver," Gem replied.

"So be it," Jat growled. His head fell back, and his mouth opened wide. A funnel of air rose from deep in his throat and burst out of his mouth, spinning into a torrent of wind, which turned into a tornado. The wind wailed and shook the building to its foundations. Jat's body dropped down, elongating the torrent into a tornado filling the building. The Circle jumped back from the edge of the hole to avoid being sucked in.

"What do we do now?" TJ shouted across the din.

"The tornado must be reversed," Gem said in a loud voice. "Otherwise, it will drain all the consciousness out of Los Angeles like a vacuum and absorb the life of the city, just as we saw on the time track."

"How do we do that?"

"Don't let the tornado drop below the ground."

"An explanation would be nice…"

No explanations came from Gen. An aura of gold light flashed around her like a supernova. She jumped feet first through the hole in the floor and disappeared into the mouth of the tornado. Dora followed in another flash of light.

The rest of the Circle was left in shock. "We don't have the full Circle," Dean said. "Willet isn't here."

"Will *is* here," Audrey said. "She spoke to me."

The tornado screamed as if it wanted to swallow them. It was spinning clockwise and dropping down inch by inch toward the floor of the building.

Dean tried to be heard over the noise of the wind. "Gem said we can't let it drop. I'm guessing that means it could drill down into the Underworld."

"What can we do to stop it?" TJ shouted back. "It's a tornado."

Dean drew the Circle around him and spoke directly into their ears. "We create an energy screwdriver and turn it the other way, into reverse."

"An energy screwdriver?" TJ said. "Interesting thought. The how is lacking. And why are you staring at me?"

Dean was indeed squinting at him. "Uh, TJ, there's a lump on your cheek." He pointed. "It's moving."

TJ probed his face with his fingers. "Oww. There's something under my skin. What is that?"

"It's turning purple," Audrey said. "The skin is breaking open! Eww! It's – a worm!"

Dean took Audrey by the shoulders. "You've got one on your chin. There's another one on your neck." He tried to wipe the worms off with both hands.

"Dean, stop it!" she said, pushing his hands away and stepping away from him.

"They broke through your skin, Audrey!"

Lumps rose on her arms, turned purple, and broke open. Blood trickled out of each lump and released a worm. They were brown, a half inch long and as big around as a child's pinkie. She wiped them off with frantic hands. When she felt them on her face, she became hysterical. "They're all over me! They're on you too, Dean!"

Worms were burrowing out through their skin as fast as they could be brushed off, leaving bloody holes and torn flesh. Blood ran in trails over their skin. The feeling of cold, slimy things slithering under their clothes became so unbearable, they stripped off their clothing, including shoes, and stood naked. Worms crawled all over them. They brushed them off frantically, but there was more. Blood oozed from the holes in their flesh and dripped on the floor.

"If we lose too much more blood, we'll faint," Audrey exclaimed. "Why is this happening?"

"We're experiencing our own decay," TJ said, looking down at his body in disgust. "Just like Jat said." He started coughing.

Audrey wiped worms off her lips with the back of her hand. "I didn't think he meant it *literally*," She bent over and retched.

Dean grabbed her around the waist and pounded her back. Blood mixed with saliva and worms streamed from her mouth. When nothing more came, she gasped. "I feel worms in my lungs."

TJ gagged up mucous and worms. Blood dripped out of his nose and down his chin. "They're eating us from the inside out."

Dean tried to clear his throat. It turned into a coughing fit. He spit out mouthfuls of a bloody mess until he caught his breath. "We don't have much time."

Worms were eating into their bellies and bowels. They doubled over, groaning in pain. Soon, their hearts would fill with worms and explode. It would be a slow, painful death. They had to make a choice while they still had one. A silent agreement was reached between them.

Streaks of blood and tears ran down Audrey's cheeks. "I love you guys." Her knees buckled.

TJ caught her arm and held her up. "You're a warrior, Audrey. We never would have made it this far without you."

"Love you both," Dean said. "Like family. Gem always says Soul never dies. Time to test that. Let's do this while we still can."

They held each others' hands despite the slime and worms on their skin. Worms squiggled between their fingers, but the love in their eyes for each other said everything that needed to be said. Leaving a life behind was never an easy decision, no matter how urgent. With a brief HU and a gulp of courage, Dean and TJ helped Audrey to the edge of the hole in the floor, and they all jumped into the mouth of the tornado. Their light bodies floated free and their failing physical shells were released to the wind and the worms.

Chapter 14

The windshear inside the tornado was ferociously strong. It howled like a banshee. The walls of the funnel-shaped vortex streaked around the Circle in ribbons of black and white that looked smooth as glass. If one was foolish enough to stick a hand or foot into the wall, the limb would be torn off, but none of them had physical limbs. They were in light bodies now. That was the only way to survive inside the vortex.

Gem and Dora hovered in the center of the swirling funnel. Willet's light body floated beside them, her blue eyes wide and luminous as a fish underwater. Audrey, Dean and TJ floated down to join them. No point speaking out loud. No one could hear a word, but their thoughts rang clear to each other. Everyone was thinking the same thing. *How do we reverse this tornado?*

Audrey spun a glowing ring of energy over her head. Dean reached up and touched it, and then TJ added his hand. When Willet touched it, the ring blazed. Gem added her hand to the ring. It flared out to the circumference of the funnel. Shafts of light connected each of them with the rim of the ring like a spoked wheel in full spin within the vortex. It pressed against the walls, digging in with a metallic squeal and exerted a counterclockwise brake against the clockwise motion of the vortex. The Circle strained to hold the wheel in place. If the tornado sunk to the ground and broke through the floor of the building, they would lose control of it. As they witnessed on the future time track, the building would descend into the Underworld, pulling everything in L.A. with it. Jat's burning black eyes flashed at them from every direction, watching them struggle,. His malicious laugh filled the vortex. The intensity of his spite seeped into their consciousness like a bitter poison, trying to dim the light of their Souls. He would know if their control of the wheel was breaking. The tornado spun harder and faster against the wheel's counterclockwise spin, an inexorable force that would not be denied.

The Circle was overmatched, and they knew it. Desperate thoughts pinged between them. "I can't hold on." "Our light is failing." They were close to the State of Despair.

"There is still light in this city," Gem's voice echoed in their thoughts. "Those Souls must lend their strength to this fight, or we are finished."

She sang a loud, chiming HU like a clarion call, and the rest of the Circle joined in. Dora lent her voice in a long coyote howl. Souls in Los Angeles that still held on to their connection with Spirit heard the call for help. Hundreds of twinkling lights dropped through the roof into the tornado's mouth and attached themselves to the wheel, lending their energy in a last-ditch effort to save their city.

The tornado howled with the ferocity of a wild beast fighting for its life. HU chants rose to answer it. The wheel flashed and burned into the walls of the vortex, resisting the clockwise turn. The air vibrated with the hum of the HU, and the tornado screamed against the resistance of the wheel. The eternal struggle between good and evil in the physical world played out in sound.

The tornado groaned, and its spin began to slow. Fire and smoke belched up from far below. A churning boil of wind swirled up and swamped the wheel. Jat's curses rang out. The enormous head of a black dragon appeared in the smoke, thrashing in the vortex with fire in its eyes. Its long leathery neck unfurled. With a roar, it opened wide its fanged jaws and blasted the wheel, swamping the Circle with flames. The dragon would destroy their connections.

It was time for the Hound of Hell to do what she was destined to do. "Go now, Dora," Gem said. "Take him down before he devours us."

The star on Dora's forehead radiated white light. Her body bristled and swelled in size, and her ferocious roar warred with the wail of the vortex. She leaped on the dragon's back with her fur smoking and clamped her jaws into its neck. Her claws buried deep in its chest. The dragon jerked and wrenched but could not shake the Hound's grip. Dora hung onto the dragon's neck, ripping into it with savage teeth, until the dragon's head hung by a tendon, its mouth still moving. Its long neck drooped backward. Dora chewed the tendon in two. The head separated from the body and dropped down into the funnel, out of sight. The rest of the dragon's body dissolved in a cloud of smoke.

Voices clamored from the wheel. "Is he gone? Is it over?" "Something's happening down there!"

Another manifestation of Jat was already taking shape in the smoke.

The tall man in the black suit replaced the dragon. His head and neck emerged from the vortex on massive shoulders and long torso. Dora climbed his back. He reached his long arms up and grabbed her, buried his taloned fingers into her ribs, and tried to rip her off his back. The Hound struggled between his hands, biting at the long taloned fingers, refusing to let go. She grew even bigger and expelled Jat's talons from her body. Her fur burned with blue fire. Eyes flashing and teeth snapping, Dora turned her white-hot breath on Jat and set his long black hair ablaze.

Jat howled in rage. "You will not stop me, Hound, not this time. I am too strong." Despite his words, his face began to melt.

The two enormous titans of the Underworld battled with legendary fury. They ripped at each other with claws and fangs. Bellows and growls and curses rang, echoing up to the rafters of what was left of the roof. Jat screamed with mouth wide open, ready to sink his black teeth into her, but the Hound was quick. In a flash, her claws grabbed his exposed throat. and breathed a torrent of scorching breath into his open mouth. Flames exploded out of Jat's ears and out the back of his head. His eyes turned liquid and ran down his cheeks. His forehead caved in. Dora climbed on his massive shoulders and bit through the back of his neck. Jat's long black tongue slithered between his lips, and his scream shattered glass throughout the building. His head fell forward, heavy and lifeless. Dora dove down toward the tail of the tornado, dragging the Deceiver's body with her, and they disappeared into the depths.

Seconds later the sound of stone cracking echoed up from far below. Growls and screams followed and then smoke billowed up through the building's core. Jat's tornado groaned to a halt and reversed into sluggish counterclockwise rotation under the relentless pressure of the wheel. The Dragon Head Building shuddered.

"Release the wheel," Gem's voice rang out.

The wheel of light retracted from the vortex walls, floated free, and melted away. Tornado winds died. In its place, a dark shadow rose. The voice of Jat came from the shadow, quieter and without its former bravado. "I am the knife's edge," he said in a monotone, as if reciting from a book, "the scourging fire, the gateway. The journey to the All in All begins with me. Until we meet again, Guardian." The voice faded, and Shadow surrendered to Light.

The light bodies of the city people who had joined the fight floated up through the broken roof of the Dragon Head Building and hovered in the sky like fireflies. They darted away, leaving the Circle to rest in the silence.

"What did he mean?" Willet's voice said after a while. "What gateway?"

"Even Jat serves the purpose for which he was created," Gem said. "To test Souls. Under his tests, Souls build strength. With strength, Souls can approach the All in All."

In the sky above the Dragon Head Building, unsettled clouds raced by, driven by strong winds, as if anticipating a change in the weather. The clouds dispersed and revealed a pure shade of blue sky that sapphires would envy. An intense golden glow beamed from a sun somewhere out of view. The sound of distant ocean waves rolled and crashed on an unseen shore. A deep, abiding peace filled their hearts.

Gem's voice rose over the din. "Welcome to the High Astral."

*****

From the street, it looked like the Dragon Head Building was having a conniption fit. The massive structure shook so violently that the crack of cement sounded like gunfire. Tomasek and Jain lifted the body of Nick Hardman. Bart and Chief Duggins picked up Willet's limp form. Edgar and Rollie took the boys by the hand, and everyone ran for the trucks. If the building fell over, they had to be much farther from it than they were.

When they were well away down the street, Rollie looked back. The shaking building was almost a blur. "I thought I'd seen everything," he said between gasps of breath. "This is a new level of insanity."

"TJ said they had to destroy the building," Tomasek said, nodding as he watched. "I guess they're doing it."

A State of Illumination

Audrey, Willet, TJ and Dean soared through the sapphire sky of the High Astral in their light bodies like birds on the wing, gliding over blue-gray mountain peaks and valleys etched with flowing rivers. Forests below rustled their emerald leaves in a gentle breeze. In the distance, a city of sparkling white stone peeked out above a high valley. Beacons of light streamed from its gold domes and spires. Memories of darkness were no match for the brilliant light and jewel-toned colors of this place. They were sure they were in some level of Heaven, but questions still lingered.

"What will happen to the building?" Audrey asked. "And all the people in the city?"

"Jat's stronghold will revert to the elements of its creation and cease to exist as a physical structure," Gem said. "The people are safe for now."

"Where are we going?" Willet said. "Not that I'm in a hurry. This is lovely."

"Augustus awaits you in Samhasa."

"It's about time we met him," TJ said with the tinge of a scowl in his voice. "We've been working for him for over a year."

"I'm in no condition to meet anyone, least of all Augustus," Dean said. "I need a shower and a month of sleep," he added, despite the fact he had no physical body to wash or rest.

They drew closer to the sparkling city and hovered over it, looking down on its streets. There were people walking, dressed in all manner of garb. It looked like any other city, but much cleaner.

A man's voice rang out like a silver bell. "I welcome you to Samhasa, dear ones."

The Circle flew down to the glowing city, drifting slowly toward a building of glittering stone with a rose garden beside it. They glided through open double doors into a large light-filled room where a white-haired man stood beside a desk made of a transparent material. He wore a light blue suit and open-collared white shirt, and his feet were bare. Here, at long last, was Augustus himself, the namesake of their Circle. The light around him was pure white and vibrated with love so profound that their hearts ached with the desire to love him in return. Love beyond words. They could barely look at him. A map of the world splattered with blotches of color hung in the air in the middle of the room. Augustus waved them in and gestured at the map. He pointed to the outline of California. The map zoomed in on the area around L.A.

"Dark clouds of emotion are clearing, thanks to the work of the Circle. The people of your city will see Light again," he said with a smile. Happiness lit his face. It was difficult not to return the smile. "The four of you put aside your own lives and personal goals to fight for others and by doing so, turned the forces of the Deceiver against him. That is true service."

"Will the people remember what happened?" Willet asked.

"What people remember of recent events will depend on their state of consciousness. Some will awaken as from a deep sleep, remembering nothing. Others will remember parts of it as in a dream. Still others, the most aware, will remember everything."

"The city is a mess," TJ said. "All they have to do is look around."

Augustus straightened the collar of his shirt. "Events on earth pass like clouds before the sun," he said. "The future is yet to be written. You have given people the opportunity to choose a different future. They would not have it if Jat prevailed."

"Sir, I meant no disrespect before," Dean stuttered. "I just don't feel – presentable. Cobwebs all over me, spider spit, worms. I'm gross."

Augustus looked him up and down. "You retain the sensations of your physical body, even though you no longer have one. Your light body needs no apologies. It looks quite presentable to me."

Dean looked down at himself and saw his body was bathed light, beautiful and perfect. Whatever travails his physical body endured, they were no longer with him. New strength surged through his being. "What will the Circle do now?" he asked.

"There must always be a Circle and a Guardian to lead them. The silent service of Souls like you has preserved civilizations on earth over the ages when there was no other hope. That being said, the future of the Circle depends upon what the Deceiver will do next. He does not act on the timescale of the physical world. It may be eons before he is seen again. Or it may be moments."

"So, the Circle might not be needed?" TJ said. "Are we disbanded?"

"Evolved is a better word." Augustus gestured to Gem. "As Guardian of the Gate in Los Angeles, our Gem demonstrated exceptional creativity and leadership in the service of Spirit against the force of darkness. This has earned a promotion with new responsibilities. Gem will assume the role of Guardian of the Gate for California. The Golden State needs her vision and devotion now more than ever."

Gem no longer wore her usual knee-length skirt and ruffled white blouse. She was now dressed in a gold silk dress with embroidered green vines running from shoulders to hem bearing red and pink flowers. Her brown eyes sparkled and her brown skin glowed. She radiated light and looked so beautiful, the Circle could only gaze at her in awe.

"What about Dora?" Willet said. "She isn't lost, is she?"

Augustus smiled. "The estimable Dora will serve at the Guardian's side as always."

The big black dog trotted through the open door from the rose garden and crossed the office to Gem. Dora glowed with vigor, and light pulsed from the white star on her forehead. Gem sank to her knees and wrapped her arms around the dog's chest. "Oh Dora, you are here. I could not breathe free until I saw you." Gem laid her cheek on Dora's head. Dora gave a big lolling grin and nestled against Gem's chest. A nimbus of gold light surrounded the Guardian and her Hound.

Gem stood and beamed at the members of the Circle. "Your fortitude and love have saved the people of Los Angeles from a dark future. You are forever in my heart, wherever I go."

Every Circle member felt Gem's love, but Willet felt a hollow place form in her heart center when she thought that Gem might leave them. The Guardian had become a constant in her life, a warm friend and a guide. The thought of losing her was so distressing that she didn't quite catch the next words Augustus spoke.

"We will need a new Guardian in Los Angeles to assist Gem and help the city heal," he continued. "A Guardian-in-Training must rise from the ranks of the Circle. I appoint our Listener to that role."

"Wait, what?" Willet stuttered as the words sunk in. "Me? I can't be a Guardian. I'm nothing like Gem!"

Augustus gave her a kind smile. "My dear, you underestimate yourself. Your ability to hear what others cannot has been a challenge for you, but you have found ways to turn it into a strength, which is much to your credit. In addition, you are the only member of the Circle with a reliable ability to move out of the physical body. This is an essential skill for a Guardian, to travel freely between worlds and assist souls on both sides of the Gate. You are uniquely qualified, Listener. Congratulations."

"No. This can't be... I'm not worthy to follow in Gem's footsteps. Who could? I'm just a girl with weird ears who used to hide in a closet to avoid migraines." Her voice cracked, her light wavered, and then it blinked out. She faded from their midst.

"What happened to my sister?" Audrey said and gave Augustus a sharp look.

TJ waved his arms through the space Willet's light had just filled. "Yeah. Where'd she go?"

"The Listener has returned to her physical body where I am sure she is thinking about her new assignment. The support of the Circle will be needed as she adjusts to her expanded duties."

"How can we help her?" TJ asked. "*We're* dead, right?"

"Do you feel dead?" Augustus asked.

TJ and Dean looked at each other and at their own light bodies. "I feel great," TJ said. "Never better," Dean added.

"Soul is eternal and free," Augustus said. "What you do now is up to you." He turned to Audrey. "Ring Thrower, what future will you choose for yourself?"

Audrey's light body flushed a pale rose. "This is Heaven, isn't it? I don't think I belong here. I killed a man. I didn't mean to, but I did. I can't stay in Heaven if I did that, right?"

"You killed someone?" TJ and Dean both exclaimed. "Who?"

"Matt Gregg. After he sic'd the spider on Dean, he threw razor blades at me, trying to cut me up. I couldn't rescue Dean without getting past him, so I threw a ring, and it sliced through his neck. It wasn't my intention, but his head fell off. Sorry if you still considered him a friend, TJ. It was self-defense, no matter what the Stone Lords said." She gave everyone a defensive glare. "I'm sorry."

"That ass and his razor blades," TJ said with a guilty glance at Augustus for his language. "I'm the one who should be sorry. Matt and I had issues. It should have been me who dealt with him. He fell for Jat's promises of power and wasn't really his human self anymore. I might have pushed him over the edge."

"I was the one who killed him." Audrey hung her head. "Can't escape that fact. And I should have killed the spider sooner, but I didn't until it was too late to save Nick Hardman. That's on me too."

"Ending the physical life of another is a serious act," Augustus said. "It is a step not taken lightly. To stay one's hand should never cause regret. In both cases, you did what you thought was right to protect yourself and your loved ones. As for the Stone Lords, the Deceiver uses them to foster a sense of guilt in vulnerable souls, to weaken them. You were right to reject their judgement."

"Well, I feel like crap, pardon my language, your grace," Audrey said, unable to meet his eyes. "I can't get over Nick's death. If I eliminated that horrible spider when I had the chance, he wouldn't have ended up wrapped in spider webs."

"Do not berate yourself, Ring Thrower. Mr. Hardman was on his own life path. Nothing happens to us that is not meant for our future."

Audrey wasn't comforted. "I'm not sure I should even throw rings anymore. I have no confidence that I'm doing the right things. What if I hurt someone by mistake? Why was I the Ring Thrower anyway?"

"The Ring Thrower focuses the energy of the Circle. You have a particular skill to unify. This is your instinct. That is why *you* are the Ring Thrower. The Deceiver tried to undermine your unifying influence by sowing doubts and discontent in your mind. He almost succeeded, but you overcame his suggestions. What's more, you challenged the spider, one of his oldest and most lethal manifestations. The success of the Circle would not have been possible without your courage."

Audrey's light body blushed pink again. "I did what I could."

"I have the same question," Dean said. "Why was I drafted into this Circle? I don't have a special ability. I'm just a drummer from Manhattan Beach."

"Your strength and integrity recommend you, and your love defines you as a Golden-Hearted Warrior. It is no mistake that you are a member of this Circle."

Dean gave Augustus a wide-eyed, confused stare. "What do I do now?"

"What would you like to do?" Augustus asked.

"I need to know my mother and brother are safe."

Augustus nodded. "That is why you are the Golden-Heart Warrior of this Circle. You care for others. You have a history, over many lifetimes, of putting the needs of others before your own."

"Many lifetimes, like reincarnation?"

"Yes."

"How do I know that? I've never been aware of any other life but this one."

"A record of past lives exists in the archives of the Third Plane. If you want this knowledge, you can go back and see for yourself. You may wish to start in Rome, in the year 2 BC. You were a Roman soldier in that life. When the Roman government began to persecute Christians, you tried to help those people. Many survived because of you."

"How do *you* know that? Did you read about me in the archive?"

"I was Guardian of the Gate in Rome at that time. We met."

"No way."

"The past exists for our review, if we need it to resolve issues in this life," Augustus replied. "But be forewarned. It is not always pleasant to behold. You may see things that disturb you. The purpose in seeing them is to understand the way you are now, not to celebrate your own past glories or lament past mistakes. Our choices of the past were not always the most noble, but they are consequential. They make us who we are today."

"Is my life as Dean Simmons over?"

Augustus smiled that warm smile that lit up the room. "All paths are open. The choices are up to you."

Dean looked at Audrey. "Where are you going, love?"

"I need to see about Willet," Audrey said. "She'll need my help. I can't abandon her now. She needs her Circle, like Gem did."

"Can I check on my mom and brother first? It's driving me crazy not to know how they are. Then we can go back together and help her."

Audrey closed her eyes "I need to feel like myself again. Gem took me to a waterfall once, somewhere around this city. The water was so wonderful and delicious. I drank it, and it healed me totally. I need that healing. Just for a little while." She turned to Dean. "You need it too. Think of all we've been through. Come with me, Dean. Let's start our journey there."

"We have asked much of you in this mission," Augustus said. "If you wish to seek your healing, you have earned the right. The living water will rejuvenate you both."

Dean took Audrey's hand in his. "Healing water sounds great. You and me. Let's go."

As Audrey visualized the waterfall and focused on it, their light bodies faded into the light of the astral sun.

That left TJ standing with Augustus and Gem. His usual air of self-confidence had deserted him. He shuffled his feet and avoided the gaze of Augustus' deep blue eyes. "Don't know why I'm here," he mumbled. "I don't do anything essential in the Circle. I'm nothing special."

"You are far from nothing," said Gem. "I told you this before, Warrior. You are the steel spine of the Circle. It revolves around you."

Augustus put a light hand on his shoulder. "The Circle looks to you as the voice of reason. You have rescued every one of them when they were in trouble. You took a young boy under your wing and saved him from dire danger despite great pain to yourself. You overcame obstacles that would terrify others. That is why *you* are the Steel Warrior."

TJ had never felt so at a loss for an appropriate response. He shook his head. "I don't feel like any kind of warrior. I did what I had to do to save my friends. As for Jonah, that was an accident. He just appeared in my life. He needed my help."

"If you think that was an accident, then you have not been paying attention. Souls enter each other's lives for a reason. You could have left Jonah with his mother with a clear conscience, but you did not. Instead, you made a vow to protect him at all costs. It was a call to service, and you answered it."

"Evelyn couldn't deal with all the evil things happening," "Jonah might have been hurt, so I had to step in. How did you know that, anyway?"

"The bonds of love shine brightly in your light body. The boy adores you, and you love him. Also, the Listener loves you dearly. Would you abandon them?"

"What can I do for anyone now if I'm not among the living? I don't need to see past lives. I had a life in L.A. It was what I wanted, and its gone."

"Is it still what you want?" Augustus asked.

TJ thought for a moment. "Everything is different now. None of the old stuff matters. What do I do with life when I don't want anything?"

"This is a decision point for you, Warrior. You can take a new body if you wish but think about how you will use it. Do you spend your new life pursuing old desires, or will you serve life? That is your decision. You have much to offer others if you choose to do so."

TJ couldn't picture himself living the life he used to live. Real estate deals and starlets and getting ahead - it all seemed so trivial. "I love Willet. It's one of the few things I still know for sure. I need to make sure she's safe. Jonah too. His mother won't be able to handle him, the older he gets. He'll listen to me. There's also my family. I haven't seen them since I joined the Circle. It would devastate my mother if she found out I was dead. I don't want her to grieve for me. If there's a Circle, I have to be there for them. Dean is like a brother to me, and Audrey, despite being a pain in the neck sometimes, saved all our lives. Whatever they do in the future, I'll help if they need me."

"Loving your near and dear ones is a good place to begin a new life. Attend to the eternal things, the things of Spirit, and you will recognize the truth behind illusions."

"I don't know what that means, sir."

Augustus winked. "It means you may discover things of true value you never knew you wanted."

TJ had made his decision, and everything around him began to blur. Augustus and Gem stood side by side, smiling at him. They receded down a long tunnel into the distance until they disappeared from his view. He felt pressure at the top of his head and fell through streams of light. He heard the single clang of a heavy gong. A heavy feeling took hold of him, and his feet touched down on solid ground. Sand flew into his eyes and scoured his skin. He started running.

*****

Willet had also dropped back into her physical body with a thud after leaving Augustus' office. Her head swam and her ears rang. When she opened her eyes, she was laying in the front seat of a truck, her feet under the steering wheel. Wincing at the pain in her stiff neck, she raised herself to a sitting position and looked out the window. There were men standing outside the driver door. Bart was one. Rollie and Edgar were there, each holding a boy by the hand, one of whom was Jonah. Clarence Duggins stood beside them, next to a rugged blonde man with stubbled chin who looked familiar. She had forgotten his name. Her brain was jumbled. She jiggled the handle of the passenger door, opened the door open and swung her legs out, wobbling when her feet touched ground. She walked around to the driver side. "What's that noise?" she mumbled, covering her ears. "We stopped the tornado. Shouldn't be any noise."

"Don't know about that. Look there, Willet," Bart said, and pointed down the street. Several blocks away, the Dragon Head Building was in the throes of a convulsion. "The building started falling apart. All the crystal I spread around the base ate into the foundation. There's nothing holding the structure to the ground."

Piles of black sand accumulated around it by the second, growing higher and higher.

Willet repeated Gem's words. "The building will revert to its elements." It was made of sand all along.

"That's a lot of sand." Rollie scratched his chin. "Shouldn't be left lying around. We have to get rid of it."

"At the rate it's growing, we'd need fifty dump trucks working round the clock," Bart said. "And where would we put it?"

"Yeah, we can't just take it to the city dump. It could hurt people. Or grow another building."

"How about the ocean?"

"Not fair to the fish," Rollie said. "What about the crystal? You said it eats pollution. The sand is pollution if you ask me."

Bart gave Rollie an appraising glance and nodded. "Crystal could work, Zeemer. I'd have to grow a whole lot more of it to eat all the sand in those piles, but it's an option." He looked at Willet. "What happened in there? Where is everybody?"

She wasn't sure what to say. "Last time I saw them, they were ok…"

"You're not sure?" The expressions on Bart's face said, 'She's got a head injury.'

Willet tried to clarify. "We had a meeting in Samhasa. It's, uh, far from here." Her head started to ache trying to find words to explain the incredible. "I had to leave early, so not sure what happened after that. I'm too tired to explain right now. Maybe later." She didn't know what else to say. The pain in her head moved into her heart as she thought of her sister, of Dean, and TJ. She pictured their faces and felt like crying. It was a miserable feeling to be disconnected from them, but she wasn't the only one in distress.

James Jain sat slumped on a nearby curb next to a body-shaped mound covered by a coat. He stared straight ahead, eyes empty, so unlike his usual animation. A shiny residue of tears streaked his cheeks. Tomasek walked over and sat down near him. Jain remained stone-faced, and the Major didn't try to start conversation.

"Bart," Willet whispered. "Who's under the coat?"

"Jain's friend, Nick Hardman," Bart said.

"Oh no, that poor man!" Willet said. "What happened?"

"We think he had a heart attack. Jain and Tomasek carried him out of the building. He was already dead."

Willet remembered the room full of webs, the bodies wrapped in silk threads, the awful silence and palpable terror, and understood how it might happen. It was an experience that could give anyone a heart attack.

"We're going to hold a service for him," Bart said. "Least we can do, and it might help Jain."

It was decided that Rollie Zeemer would lead them in the Lord's Prayer, and then Major Tomasek would preside, since Nick was former military. When the service commenced, the small group of mourners gathered around Nick's body. There was no grassy place for him, so he lay on the sidewalk. Tomasek took off his own U.S. flag pin and pinned it on Nick's jacket. He spoke words appropriate for a man who had served his country with distinction and died trying to protect a young boy. Members of the Circle not with them were included in the words.

"Heroes unknown to others stand against danger and

impossible obstacles to serve and protect their fellow men. We salute them. Help us not to mourn those who have died in service, but rather to gain strength from the fact that such heroes have lived."

Tomasek, Duggins, and Edgar Zeemer stood beside Nick's body and held a military salute. Bart and Rollie placed hands over their hearts, and the young boys bowed their heads. Jain cried like a broken man who had lost a brother and a friend.

Willet had never felt so desolate. She held Jain's hand through the ceremony and hugged him close when it was over. The three people most dear to her were so far away. She knew the overwhelming emptiness he must feel. There was discussion of a burial, but she couldn't focus on it. She heard a voice asking her a question. It was Bart. What was he saying?

"Willet, what's going on? Where's Audrey? Dean and TJ. They're coming back, aren't they? And Gem?"

She couldn't say the word out loud. Death. It didn't mean the same thing to her that it once did, but she knew what it would mean to Bart. "They're away, out of body, Bart," she said, searching his eyes for a glimmer of understanding. "We won't see them again, maybe for a while, but they're ok. Just - not here." Her tears started to flow, and she couldn't stop them.

Bart wrapped an arm around her shoulders. "Oh," he said. "Oh no." He was shaking.

She felt his tears on her hair. It made her bury her face against his shoulder. Bart knew. They both ached for lost love and held each other up to keep from collapsing. Then the silence was broken.

"Well, speak of the devil," Edgar said.

"Mr. Tom, Mr. Tom!" Jonah shouted and broke into a run.

Willet and Bart turned to look up the street. A tall figure ran toward them with a long loping stride and black sand on his shoulders. He wiped sand out of his eyes and brushed it off his hair as he approached. Tomasek and Bart sprinted toward him. They clapped him on the back and shook his hand. "You made it, man," they said. "It's a miracle." Even Edgar walked up to shake his hand.

Jonah reached TJ and jumped up and down in front of him. "I knew you wouldn't leave us," he said. "I knew you'd come back." He threw his arms around TJ's waist

TJ pulled him closer. "Boy, you've grown since I last saw you. It's only been an hour."

Willet ran too. When she reached him, she threw her arms around his neck. Her voice trembled and broke. "Thomas. You're here," she said. "I thought I'd never…"

TJ hugged her under his arm. "Of course, I'm here," he replied. "Did you think I'd leave the Guardian in training without backup?" He whispered in her ear. "I don't pretend to understand how it's possible. What's happening to the building?"

"The place destroyed itself," she said. "We gave it a swift kick in the right direction." She wiped dust off his cheeks and lips and kissed him.

"Mr. Tom," Jonah said, "Where did you come from? You were in the sand."

Willet noticed a shimmer of light on his skin. "You're sparkling," she murmured. "Just like Gem when she - came back after Theese shot her." She gave a sidelong glance at Jonah, not wanting to recall the specifics of the shooting in front of him, but she had to know.

"Yeah this is a new chassis. Looks the same as the old one, right?" He smiled.

"Yes, but why?"

TJ didn't spare the details. "Worms ate my physical body from the inside out while I was still in it," he said. "Same for Audrey and Dean. It was so disgusting, we jumped into the tornado just to get rid of the slimy feeling. Those bodies were toast anyway. There was no going back to them."

Her worst fear prickled under her skin. "Where are Dean and Audrey? Are they…coming back too?"

"Don't know, babe. I really don't. They're taking a spa vacation at some healing waterfall. Your sister was pretty torn up. What happened with Matt Gregg, with Nick, the spider and the worms. It messed with her head in a serious way. She needs to put herself back together mentally and emotionally. The waterfall will help both of them, I hope."

"So, they'll rest and come back…"

"Dean said something about a trip to Rome."

"Oh. Rome." Willet sounded deflated. "That's nice. A vacation is good I guess."

"I mean Rome in the year 2 B.C.E."

"*Ancient* Rome? No way. Rome was a brutal place back then. Why would he go there?"

"It's more of a spirit quest than a vacation." TJ gave a side-glance at Jonah who was squint-eyed with confusion at the turns in the conversation. "Now it's all about you, Guardian."

"How can I be a Guardian without my sister?" Audrey was the ultimate constant in Willet's life. With both Gem and Audrey gone, the sense of loss was crushing. "She has to come back. I need her!" Tears started falling all over again. It felt like she might never be able to stop.

TJ held her close and tried to dry those tears off her cheeks with his shirt. He didn't want to say much in front of Jonah. "We'll stay calm and figure something out. I know Audrey is worried about you too. Augustus told all of us we had choices. When she feels better, she'll make one." The blood stains on Willet's ears drew his attention. "What's the explanation for this?" he said, examining her ears. "You have blood on your ears."

She sniffled and tried to rub away the blood with the sides of her hands. "Oh that. A present from Jat. He blew my ear drums out. I'm slowly getting my hearing back."

"I hope Dora ripped him apart," he snarled and planted a fierce kiss on her forehead.

Willet had little concern for her ears. The lump in her throat was hard as stone. Would she ever see her sister again? She thought of all their silly spats and cross words. What a waste of time. And Dean – she loved him like a brother. She never told him how much she appreciated his steady friendship and kindness. There couldn't be a Circle without Audrey and Dean. Fortunately TJ was by her side, the love of her life, and that was a miracle. She wasn't completely alone. She threw her arms around his neck again and hugged him like she'd never let go.

"We deserve a break too, Will," TJ murmured in her ear. "How about this idea? I know a little café near Notre Dame de Paris that bakes *the* most perfect croissants. Buttery, flaky, you'll never forget them. Allow me to accompany you to Paris, mademoiselle. Just for a couple days. We'll come back and take care of Circle business after that."

Willet thought wistfully of the City of Lights. "I've always wanted to see Paris," she said, "but what if L.A. is overrun again? I'm supposed to protect the people."

As always, Paris was a mirage eluding her. Does a Guardian ever take a vacation, even a Guardian in training? She didn't remember Gem taking one. Circle business meant dealing with the glittering remnants of Red Souls still flying through the streets. Jat's noisy minions were left high and dry when the Dragon Head Building collapsed. They sounded angry, screaming about why their great leader had abandoned them. When people returned to the streets, Red Souls would attack them with a vengeance. Dark thoughts would be planted in people's minds all over again. Rage and violence might rise. Someone had to sweep Red Souls through the Astral Gate, back to the Underworld, and shut the Gate. That was her job now. She had no idea how she would do it. The worry made her head hurt even more.

I don't have Gem's Freezing Breath. All I can do is listen. Listening isn't exactly an offensive weapon. There has to be something more, some other skill I can learn to fight the nasties like Gem did.

TJ folded her into his arms. In the warm depth of their embrace, realities were kept at bay that would soon have to be faced. "You need a rest, girl. *We* need a break."

She *was* deeply tired. There had to be a way. "How about a quicker getaway? Maybe twenty-four hours?"

He smiled at her, smoothed back the damp blonde curls from her forehead. "The Traveler will be busy escorting Dean around Rome. Her taxi service may not be available to take us across the ocean on short notice."

"Well then," she smiled back. "I'll have to teach you how to travel out-of-body."

"Can we eat French croissants?"

"Unfortunately, no, but we can watch the sun rise over the Seine and see the Eiffel Tower light up at night."

"Hmm. Will close work between student and teacher be required?"

She rose up on her toes and kissed him softly on the lips. "Oh yes," she said. "Very close."

A State of Transition

After the memorial service for Nick Hardman, the group of individuals who worked together to defeat Jat the Deceiver began to think about going their separate ways. They exchanged phone numbers and email in case such services were restored in L.A. There were hugs and farewells all around. Edgar clutched his son to his side, with tears in his eyes, and shook everyone's hand. Bart and Rollie declared firm and lasting friendship for each other. Chuck Tomasek and TJ acknowledged each other as brothers in battle, a bond that could never be broken.

As acting Guardian of Los Angeles, it was Willet's place to address the team. "Thank you all," she said. "You saved the people of this city from a grave outcome. We couldn't have succeeded without you. You are truly heroes, and our friends, always."

James Jain didn't speak to anyone after the service. His face was a mask of rigidly controlled pain as Nick's body was placed in Edgar's truck so it could be taken to the city morgue. As police chief, that was Edgar's job. When no one was looking, Jain snuck into the truck, drove off and disappeared into the L.A. streets he knew so well. Edgar was not happy. He would have to track down the vehicle thief, recover the body, and take Jain into custody, but he reluctantly agreed not to arrest him unless Jain went off the deep end and did something crazy.

Rollie had to get back to his family and his business. He gave his good bye and drove off with Robbie in Rollie's car. He would return the boy to his mother. Major Tomasek saluted one and all, found his own truck and took off to wherever he came from. That left Bart, Willet, TJ and Jonah standing in the street in view of the growing mountain of black sand.

"Jonah," TJ said. "We have to get you back to your mother."

"I don't want to go," Jonah said. "I want to stay with you."

"She's worried sick by now, boy. You're too young to be away from her."

"I'm thirteen," the boy said defiantly, "and I had a spider on top of me." His skin drained of color. He fought back tears. "The spider put its creepy feet on my face. It had huge eyes and fangs…". He stopped to catch his breath. "That other kid, Robbie, he was crying, but I didn't cry. I can fight like you, Mr. Tom. I want to fight monsters like you do, so they don't hurt people. So, they can't hurt me." He was trembling.

Jonah had faced a terrible nightmare. He might suffer night terrors for years, maybe his whole life. What could they do for him? "Buddy," TJ said, "we can't take a thirteen-year-old boy away from this mother without her permission. We could be accused of kidnapping."

Jonah's eyes pleaded. "If you leave me with her, I'll just run away. She can't protect me. You're the only one who can. You and Ms. Willet."

Bart offered a suggestion to keep the peace. "Last time we saw your mom, she was at Griffith Park with Arhat. We should go see if she's still there. If she is, you can ask her if it's ok to spend some time with TJ. How about that?"

TJ and Willet welcomed the idea. "Yes, that's what we need to do," they said, looking relieved. Jonah didn't look too happy, but he couldn't offer a rebuttal. They all piled into Bart's truck. The front seat was a cozy fit. Willet sat on TJ's lap, and Jonah sat in the middle with arms crossed over his chest in a show of displeasure with the whole idea of being returned to his mother like a baby.

As they headed to Griffith Park, they got a good view of the city now that the Dragon Head Building was reduced to sand. The cracked streets merely smoked instead of flamed. People stood stock-still, their eyes wide and staring, as if they were shell-shocked. The atmosphere changed colors, black to gray to green to yellow, back to gray, then white. Telltale wisps of red smoke floated erratically through the air. Red Souls. They were still around.

"Things feel unsettled," Willet said. "It will take a while for the city to get back to normal."

The subject of transportation came up. TJ and Willet had no wheels. "We lost every vehicle we owned among the four of us," TJ said. "My truck was confiscated by the LAPD, and the Mercedes got left on the road to Mount Wilson. Who knows if it's still there? Dean's truck went off a cliff in the mountains."

Willet added her own list of losses. "Audrey's Porsche was totaled when she ran into a block of crystal. I think our Beemer got carjacked. Gem's Jeep was thrashed by falling boulders when we drove it out of the mountains. It's not drivable in its current condition. What are we going to do?"

"Well, there's nothing more pressing that I have to do," Bart said. "Consider me your taxi service until you can find something to drive."

TJ put a hand on Bart's shoulder. "You're a good man, Bart. Thank you. We're in your debt."

"You don't owe me anything. You guys saved L.A. I don't know how you did it, but I know you did. You stopped what was going on in that building. I can't imagine what that was like."

There wasn't much traffic, and the drive to Griffith Park proceeded mostly in silence. It was nice just to relax and not be in a State of Panic under threat of impending doom. They reached the Park and drove up the forested drive, surprised to see that the trees were still leafy green as if nothing had happened. The Park seemed untouched by the traumas that hit the city. When they got to the concourse in front of the Observatory, they parked and walked around, but not a soul was there. Everyone got out. TJ called Evelyn's name, then Arhat's. No voices answered.

"See," Jonah said happily, "Mom's not here. That means I can stay with you, right?"

Again, it was hard to argue. They couldn't leave Jonah in the Park alone so they got back in the truck and headed for the exit. Next stop – Pine Siskin House. That was a long drive east to the desert. Jonah nodded off. Willet laid her head on TJ's shoulder and sighed a contented sigh.

The Wall of Unknowing was shredding apart and blowing away in tatters. Shafts of lightning cracked here and there, but sunlight had broken through the remnants of the darkness. When people saw the sun, they stared as if they'd never seen it before. By the time Bart pulled up to the circular drive at Pine Siskin House, the sun hovered over the western horizon, filling the sky with streaks of red and gold. Willet slipped off TJ's lap and ran for the front door, found the key tucked behind a bronze light fixture, and unlocked the door. Everyone followed her inside. There was a hushed silence inside. The interior was cool and dark. Home. At long last, home.

Willet felt like she had been holding her breath since she left and was just now able to breathe. "Our home is your home," she said. "Bart, the guest room is yours. There's a shower in there. Jonah, there are sheets and a blanket on the day bed in the office. You'll want to take a shower too, she said, fixing him with a look in case he resisted. "There's TV in the living room, food in the kitchen. Help yourself to whatever you want."

"What are you guys doing?" Jonah asked.

"We're going to sleep. We'll see you in the morning."

She reached for TJ's hand and led him down the hallway to the back of the house, to the master bedroom. The sound of a door closing echoed with quiet finality, the sound of an ending, and a beginning.

A State of Renewal

Audrey and Dean splashed in the cool depths of a bubbling waterfall pouring into a rock pool and drank their fill of its refreshment. The water sparkled and sang like liquid music. Energy rushed through them and soothed every hurt. Birds flew overhead, chirping happily, and a gentle breeze blew. Sitting at the edge of the pool, they basked in the warmth of sunlight so pure they'd never seen or felt anything like it. There was little need for words between them.

The dull ache in Audrey's heart eased, and an exultant joy filled her. She wanted to sing, so she did, warbling random notes she never could have summoned from her physical voice. "I wish we could stay here forever," she said. "I don't want to remember or think. Just be."

Dean chuckled. "Is that even possible? Have we really earned a permanent place in heaven?"

"It doesn't matter. I have a responsibility to Willet now that she's a Guardian. We know what a big job she has. She'll need a Ring Thrower and a Golden-Hearted Warrior at her side."

Even in the joy of their refreshment and healing, there were nagging reminders of issues unresolved. Together or apart, those issues would have to be addressed. They looked into each other's eyes and recognized their feelings for each other. An aching love replaced all the other aches that had been healed.

"I haven't forgotten my commitment to the Circle," Dean said. "Or to you. That won't change, no matter what else I do. I love you, Audrey."

"I've waited so long to hear you say that. I love you too."

They embraced that truth and found themselves back in Augustus' office.

 "Feeling better?" Augustus asked.

"That felt great," Dean said. "Just what I needed."

"I do feel better," Audrey said. "But I feel kind of guilty to be this happy."

The gaze from Augustus' deep blue eyes pierced like an arrow. "Why?"

"James Jain. I owe him something. Not sure what, but he'll need help after losing Nick."

"You take this as your responsibility?"

"I guess I do."

"Then it is yours," Augustus said and turned to Dean. "I sense you have questions, Golden Heart."

Dean realized he did have a question. "There *is* something I've wondered about. Why does Los Angeles have a Guardian? Gem is amazing, of course. We couldn't do what we do without her, but there are lots of cities. Do they all have Guardians?"

Augustus nodded. "In large cities where many people live close together, there is more friction. It is fertile soil for the Deceiver to plant his negative suggestions. They spread roots into the consciousness of individuals and act like lit matches. Conflicts flare and spread. A Guardian is assigned to maintain balance. Without it, the Deceiver can do what he did in your city."

"People always have a choice though, right?" Dean said. "To not fall for the suggestions? That's what Gem says."

"In our Souls, we are free. In our minds, we make choices. In our physical bodies, we deal with the limitations around us."

"My sister will need help if she's doing Guardian work," Audrey said. "She'll need the Circle. I can't abandon her."

Augustus nodded. "Yes, she will. You can make any choice you wish as long as you are willing to accept all that comes with it."

"That sounds like a warning," Audrey said.

"Every choice has consequences. Whether good or bad depends on how we view them. It is the way of the worlds below the pure positive Soul Plane. Nothing comes to us without a cost."

"Isn't there a way to have love and do good things without a penalty?"

"There is a way. It is selfless action, the desireless way, following the guidance of Spirit in every situation without thought of self."

"I don't think I'm that good," Dean said. "There are still things I want. Love. Music. Family. I want to see my mother, and then I want to check out my life in Rome. I'd like you to come with me, Audrey."

"Your heart's desires will lead you," Augustus said. "What say you, Ring Thrower?"

It was difficult for her to admit what she was thinking. "My path is not yours, Dean, at least for now." She turned to Augustus. "Can the heart desire two things equally at the same time?"

"Yes," Augustus nodded, "But you can only follow one at a time."

Their eyes met and acknowledged that this was goodbye, for now. "Meet me at Pine Siskin House," she whispered. "When you're done wandering."

Dean took her in his arms and kissed her. "Til then, love." She returned his kiss with all the warmth and passion of her heart. Their light bodies faded from each other's arms.

Augustus watched and smiled. What the desires of their hearts truly were, they would soon discover.

A new cycle begins for the Circle of Augustus in The Listener Series.

Book 1: The Woman in the Wires

What will the Circle do now without two of its members? How will Willet handle her new position as L.A.'s Guardian of the Gate? Can she find a way to dispose of the mountain of cursed black sand that now sits in the middle of L.A.?

www.ingramcontent.com/pod-product-compliance
Lightning Source LLC
Chambersburg PA
CBHW070641180626
46817CB00006B/2188